Maggie wasn't prep
weight of Kevlar sl

Her lungs collapsed under the attack. A crack of thunder distorted Jones's voice as he ripped her off the ground and shoved her up the incline. Her heart rate rocketed into her throat. No. Not thunder. A gunshot. Someone had taken a shot at them. "They found me."

Jones was still yelling orders at her, but she couldn't hear through the high-pitched ringing in her ears. He seemed to use his body as a shield between her and the gunman as he pushed his hand into her lower back. Her leg threatened to collapse straight out from under her, but he somehow made up for the difference.

Maggie slapped her hand on flat ground as they reached the rim of the oversized crater and dug her fingernails in to get a good grip. Only she didn't have to drag herself over the lip. Jones was already pushing her upward.

"Run for the SUV, Maggie. Don't stop. Not even for me."

K-9 SHIELD

NICHOLE SEVERN

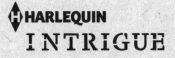

To the men and women fighting for our freedom.

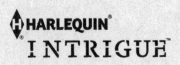

ISBN-13: 978-1-335-59152-4

K-9 Shield

Copyright © 2024 by Natascha Jaffa

Recycling programs
for this product may
not exist in your area.

This is a work of fiction. Names, characters, places and incidents are either the product of the author's imagination or are used fictitiously. Any resemblance to actual persons, living or dead, businesses, companies, events or locales is entirely coincidental.

For questions and comments about the quality of this book, please contact us at CustomerService@Harlequin.com.

TM and ® are trademarks of Harlequin Enterprises ULC.

Harlequin Enterprises ULC
22 Adelaide St. West, 41st Floor
Toronto, Ontario M5H 4E3, Canada
www.Harlequin.com

Printed in U.S.A.

Nichole Severn writes explosive romantic suspense with strong heroines, heroes who dare challenge them and a hell of a lot of guns. She resides with her very supportive and patient husband, as well as her demon spawn, in Utah. When she's not writing, she's constantly injuring herself running, rock climbing, practicing yoga and snowboarding. She loves hearing from readers through her website, www.nicholesevern.com, and on Facebook at nicholesevern.

Books by Nichole Severn

Harlequin Intrigue

New Mexico Guard Dogs

K-9 Security
K-9 Detection
K-9 Shield

Defenders of Battle Mountain

Grave Danger
Dead Giveaway
Dead on Arrival
Presumed Dead
Over Her Dead Body
Dead Again

A Marshal Law Novel

The Fugitive
The Witness
The Prosecutor
The Suspect

Visit the Author Profile page at Harlequin.com.

CAST OF CHARACTERS

Jones Driscoll—He just ended up in the middle of a war zone. Protecting a secretive journalist who fights him every step of the way pushes the combat controller to the limits, and danger is heating up—as is their mutual attraction.

Maggie Caddel—Being on the front line of the war on drugs isn't everything this war correspondent imagined. Abducted by the cartel, she's interrogated about her sources until a far-too-handsome stranger helps her escape. But soon she realizes the cartel will do whatever it takes to ensure she takes their secrets to the grave.

Socorro Security—The Pentagon's war on drugs has pulled the private military contractors of Socorro Security into the fray to dismantle the *Sangre por Sangre* cartel...forcing its operatives to risk their lives and their hearts in the process.

Sosimo Toledano—The prodigal son and heir to *Sangre por Sangre* won't stop until every last threat to the cartel is neutralized, including a war correspondent who could cost him everything he's worked for.

Scarlett Beam—The security consultant only wants one thing: for her skill set to do good in the world. She's signed on with Socorro for that exact mission, but this fight is far larger than she ever expected.

Chapter One

People were—or they became—what they pretended to be.

And Maggie Caddel had been pretending for a very long time.

Plastic cut into the sensitive skin of her wrists. She wasn't sure how long she'd been here. Getting dripped on from a leaky pipe overhead, told when she could eat, when she could stand, when to speak. Her tongue felt too big for her mouth now. Thirst did that. She'd pulled against the zip ties too many times to count. It was no use. Even if she managed to break through, there was nowhere to go. Nowhere she could run they wouldn't find her.

A thick steel door kept the animals out but kept her in. Maggie shifted away from the cinder block wall. She'd somehow managed to fall asleep, even with the echoes of shouted orders and footsteps outside her door. Another drip from above ripped her out of sleep. It splattered against the side of her face and tendrilled down her neck.

This place… It held an Aladdin's cave of secrets she'd worked the past year to uncover. But not like this.

Not at the expense of ten American soldiers dead. And not at the expense of her life. The war waging between the federal government and the New Mexico cartel *Sangre por Sangre* had already cost so much.

A metallic ping of keys twisted in the lock. Rusted hinges protested as the door swung inward. El Capitan framed himself in the doorframe. His eyes seemed to sink deeper in their sockets every time they went through their little routine. Darker than should be possible for a human. If that was what he was. Judging by his willingness to interrogate, torture and starve a random war correspondent, Maggie wasn't sure there was any humanity left.

She set her forehead back against the wall. It was starting again. The questions. The pain. She wasn't sure her legs would even carry her out of this room. "I'm guessing you didn't bring me the ice cream sandwich I asked for."

It'd been the only thing she could think of that she wanted more than anything else in the world. Other than being released.

El Capitan—she didn't know his real name—closed in. Strong hands pulled her to her feet and tucked her into his side. The toes of her boots dragged behind her, and it took another cartel soldier's aid to get her into the corridor.

The walls blurred in her peripheral vision. She'd spent the first few days memorizing everything she could. The rights and lefts they took to the interrogation room. The stains on the soldiers' boots, the rings they wore, the tattoos climbing up their necks. El Capitan, for instance, wore the same cologne day-to-day. It'd been overly spicy and would ward off demons in a pinch, but the ski mask usually hiding his face had taken some of the bite out. Given the chance, all she would've had to do was smell him to make a positive ID.

But he wasn't wearing the mask anymore.

Which meant he wasn't worried about her identifying him anymore.

Because they were going to kill her.

Both gunmen thrust her down into the chair she'd bled in for the past…she couldn't remember how many days had gone by. Three days? A week? They'd all started to stitch together without any windows in her cell to judge day or night. Like she'd been kept in a basement. But this room had a small crack in the ceiling. Enough for her to know they'd dragged her here in the middle of the night.

Maggie let the sharp back of the chair press into the knots in her shoulder blades. The wood felt as though it was swelling as it absorbed her sweat, her tears— her blood. Could crime labs pull DNA from wood? She hoped so. It would probably be all that was left of her given what she'd witnessed.

"I'm losing my patience with you." El Capitan rubbed one fist into the opposite palm. Like warming up his knuckles would make any difference against her face. "Where are the photos you took? Who did you give them to?"

Same old game. Same old results. That first day had been the hardest, when she had no choice but to be mentally present every second, to experience every ounce of pain inflicted. But now... Now she'd learned how to step out of her body. To watch from above while the Maggie below suffered at the hands of a bloodthirsty cartel lieutenant trying to clean up the mess he made. "What photos?"

The strike twisted her head over one shoulder. Lightning burst behind her eyelids. The throbbing started in her jaw and exploded up into her temple. And that was all it took. To detach. Disassociate. She wasn't in the chair anymore. Some other woman was. A part of her that was strong enough to get through whatever came next. She could stand there and observe without ever feeling that man's hands on her again.

"We've been through your home. We've been through your car. Next, we'll question everyone you care about." El Capitan was in a mood today. More hostile than usual. Desperate.

Maggie couldn't help but like that idea. That he was feeling the pressure of getting results out of her. That she'd held him off this long. The Maggie in the chair was having a hard time keeping her head up. She dropped her chin to her chest. "If you get ahold of my sister, tell her I want my green sweater back."

"You have no idea who you're dealing with, do you, little girl?" The cartel lieutenant stuck his face close to hers. Even separated from her body, she could smell the cigarettes on his breath. "What we can do to you, to your family, your life. All you have to do is give me the photos you took that night and this ends. You'll be able to go home."

Home? She didn't have a home. Didn't he realize that? All she'd done over the past two years was disappoint her friends, her family, her coworkers. Investigating *Sangre por Sangre*'s growing influence throughout the Southwest was all she had left. And she wasn't going to let them get away with what they'd done. No matter the cost.

Except no one knew she was here.

No one cared. Certainly not her ex-husband.

Not even her editor would know where to start.

No one was coming to save her.

And the photos she'd taken of that tragic night—when the cartel had slaughtered ten American soldiers and disposed of the bodies in an ambush meant to capture the cartel founder's son—would rot where she'd hidden them. Maggie licked her broken lips, not really feeling the sting anymore. Her head fell back, exposing her throat, as she tried to meet El Capitan's eyes. Sweat prickled at the back of her neck. "It's hot. Can I have that ice cream sandwich, please?"

The lieutenant fisted a handful of her hair, trying to force her to look at him, but Maggie wasn't in that body. All he was looking at was a shell. A beaten and bloodied ghost of the woman she used to be. "Take her out in the middle of the desert and leave her for the coyotes to chew on. She's worthless."

He shoved her body backward.

Gravity pitted in her stomach a split second before the Maggie in the chair hit the floor. The back of her head hit the cement, and suddenly she didn't have the strength to stay detached from that shell she'd created.

In an instant, she was right back in her body. Feeling the pain crunch through her skull, realizing the warmth spreading through her hair was blood. Her vision wavered as she tried to reach for that numbness that had gotten her through the past few days, but it wasn't there anymore. Shallow breathing filled her ears. "No. No. Don't do this. You can't do this."

"Clean that up. I want this entire room and her cell scrubbed down." El Capitan threw orders with a wave of his hand as he headed for the corridor. "Make it so no one will know she was ever here."

Two sets of hands dragged her upright. Every muscle in her body tensed in defense, but she'd lost her will to fight back days ago. It wasn't supposed to be like this. She was going to make something of herself. This story…this was supposed to change everything.

Maggie tried to dig her heels into the cement, but her added weight crumbled pieces of the floor away. Her arms hurt. This was it. Everything she'd done to rewrite her life had been for nothing. Tears burned in her swollen eyes. "Please."

The men at her sides didn't respond, didn't lighten their grip. Didn't alter their course. They pulled her through a door she hadn't known existed in the shadows until right then. One leading directly outside.

She'd been so close to escaping without ever even knowing.

A thud registered from behind her. Then another. She tried to angle her head around, but it was pointless. Pointless to hope El Capitan had charged back into the room with a change of mind. She was going to die.

A groan rumbled through her side a split second before the gunman at her left dropped to his knees. He fell forward. Unmoving. She didn't understand. The second soldier marching her to her death released his hold, and she hit the floor. Another groan infiltrated through the concentrated thud of her heart behind her ears.

Then…nothing.

For a moment, Maggie wondered if the head wound had caused damage to her hearing or her brain had short-circuited. Then she heard him.

"Don't try to move. You're badly injured, but I'm going to get you out of here." Something wet and rough licked along one of her ears. "Gotham, knock it off. Don't you think she's been through enough?"

A small whine—like a dog—replaced the sensory input at her ear. A dark outline shifted in front of her. Masked. Like El Capitan, but that wasn't… That wasn't his voice.

Maggie cataloged what she could see of his eyes through the cutouts in the fabric. She'd never met this one before. She would've remembered. Her vision wavered as a set of muscled arms threaded beneath her knees and at her lower back. He hauled her into his chest, and there wasn't a single thing she could do to stop him as darkness closed in. "You're not one of them."

SHE'D LOST CONSCIOUSNESS.

Jones Driscoll brought her against his chest, back against the wall, as he scouted for an ambush. *Sangre por Sangre*'s half-destroyed headquarters were settled at the bottom of a damn fishbowl in the middle of the freaking desert. Any number of opportunities for the cartel to take advantage. He'd managed to knock out a couple of the cartel lieutenant's direct reports back in the interrogation room, but the man of the hour had managed to escape down one of the corridors. Ivy Bardot—Socorro's founder—would give him hell for that. Months of research, of tracking Sosimo Toledano's movements, of trying to build a case for the federal government to make a move. And Jones had blown it the second he'd laid eyes on her.

He moved as fast as he dared straight out into the open. Cracked New Mexico earth threatened his balance as he headed for the incline that would take him back to his SUV. His legs burned with the woman's added weight, but Gotham wasn't helping either. The husky kept cuing his owner with every hint of human remains buried in this evil place.

Low voices echoed through the disintegrating parking garage. The structure was on the brink of collapse, yet satellite imagery and recon reported an uptick in activity over the past three days. Most recently utilized as a hideout for Sosimo Toledano, identified as *Sangre por Sangre*'s prodigal son. Heir to the entire organization, if and when the feds managed to capture the big dog. Seemed Sonny Boy was trying to make a name of his own. Ever since Ponderosa's chief of police had come back from the dead for revenge against the cartel, there'd been an increase in attacks on the small towns fighting to stay out of cartel business. Homes ransacked, residents running from public parks as gunfire broke out, businesses broken into and burned to the ground—all of it leading back to a single shot caller: Sosimo Toledano. Local police couldn't keep up with the onslaught and turned to Socorro.

But what was it about this place *Sangre por Sangre* couldn't seem to let go of? An explosion had weakened the supports months ago, the foundation was failing, water was penetrating the walls and eroding the floors. Yet the cartel lieutenant had abducted, questioned and tortured the woman in his arms. Caddel. He'd called her Ms. Caddel. No first name.

Jones backed them into the shadows at the sight of two gunmen taking a cigarette break under the overhang of the underground parking garage, staying invisible. That was his job. To get in and out of enemy territory without raising the alarm. To discern the cartel's next move and calculate their strategy before they had a chance to strike. He'd lived and thrived in combat zones for half his life, but this… He studied the outline of the woman's face highlighted by a single flare of a lighter a few feet away. This felt different. What the hell could *Sangre por Sangre* want with one woman?

Laughter ricocheted through the hollow cement darkness. One move. That was all it would take, and the soldiers would be on him. Wasn't normally a problem. He lived for the fight, to be on the front lines of defense. Just him and his opponent. Protecting a woman who'd been beaten to within an inch of her life was a whole other story. It would be hard to engage while worrying about whether or not she was still breathing.

Gotham pawed at Jones's cargo pants. A low groan signaled he'd found the scent of human remains close by.

"Shh." Pressing into Gotham's paw with one leg, Jones hoped to quiet the husky's need for attention. They were probably standing on an entire cemetery, given Toledano's recent crimes against humanity. But there wasn't anything he could do about it right now.

"You hear that?" One of the gunmen faced toward Jones's position. Though his lack of response said he hadn't spotted them yet. Too dark.

Gotham jogged to meet the nearest gunman. A low warning vibrated through Jones's throat, but the husky didn't pay him any mind. Jones adjusted his hold on the unconscious woman against his chest in case he had to make a jump for his dog.

The nearest gunman swung his rifle free from his shoulder, taking a step forward as Gotham waltzed right up to him, and a tension unlike anything Jones had experienced laced every muscle in his body. A smile broke out across both soldiers' faces, and the second took a knee, hand extended. "Where'd you come from?"

Hot damn. Gotham had provided a distraction, giving Jones the chance to get out without raising suspicions. Jones sidestepped his position, keeping to the wall as the gunmen searched for something to give the dog.

Joke was on them. Gotham only ate a certain brand of dog food and jerked pig ears.

He tightened his hold around Ms. Caddel as one of the spotlights swept across her face. Matted blond hair streaked with dirt and something like liquid rust caught in his watch. Not rust. Blood. His gut clenched as he got his first real good look at her swollen eyes, the cuts along her mouth, the bruising darkening the contours of her face. This woman had been through hell. But he was going to get her out.

Jones hiked the incline he'd descended to get into the structure. Sand dissolved beneath his weight, but he put everything he had into keeping upright with an added hundred and thirty pounds. Just a little farther. He could almost see his SUV on the other side of the barbed fence in the distance. He cleared the incline and stepped onto flat ground.

A yip pierced his senses.

The sound fried his nerves as he recognized Gotham's cry for help.

He turned back. The husky was hanging upside down by one foot in the soldier's extended hand, arcing up to bite at the man's wrist. Another series of laughs drew out a full bark from his dog. Setting Ms. Caddel down as gently as possible on flat ground, he tried to breathe through the rage mixing into his blood. He might not like being weighed down by a K9 sidekick who'd rather chase his own tail than pay attention to anything Jones had to say, but no one touched his partner.

He descended the incline, not bothering to keep to the shadows this time around. Two armed gunmen didn't stand a chance against a combat controller employed by the most-resourced security company in the world.

Surprise etched onto one gunman's face as he locked on Jones's approach. The guy unholstered a pistol at his hip and took aim.

Jones dodged the barrel of the weapon, sliding up the soldier's arm. He rocketed his fist into the gunman's throat. A bullet exploded mere inches from his ear and triggered a ringing through his skull. Grabbing onto the cartel member's neck, Jones hauled the attacker to the ground. They fell as one. He pinned the gunman's hand back by the thumb until a scream filled the night. The gun fell into Jones's hand as the second soldier lunged.

The second bullet found home just beneath the bastard's Kevlar, and the soldier dropped Gotham as his knees met the earth. The K9's yip and quick scramble to his feet let Jones know he hadn't been hurt.

Jones pressed one boot into the gunman's chest and rolled him onto his back.

"What did your boss want with her? The woman you were supposed to execute." He hiked the soldier's thumb back to increase the pressure on the tendon running up into the wrist and forearm. Once that tore, there'd be no squeezing saline solution into a contacts case or a trigger for the rest of his life. "Why take her?"

The resulting scream drowned out the ringing in his ears.

"She was there!" The cartel member shoved into his heels, trying to break away from Jones's hold, but there was no point. The harder he tried to escape, the more damage was done.

"Where?" he asked.

"I know who you are." A wheeze slid through crooked, poorly maintained stained teeth. That was the thing about cartels. Every member worked for the good of the whole, but that relationship didn't go both ways. No dental coverage. No health coverage. Just a binding promise to die for the greater good. "I know who you work for."

"Then you know I won't stop until every last one of you are behind bars." Clutching the gun's grip harder, Jones pounded his fist into the soldier's face. Bone met dirt in a loud snap that knocked the son of a bitch unconscious.

Gotham raced to Jones's feet as he shoved to stand, coming up onto his hind legs.

"This is why you're not supposed to leave my side. How many times do we have to talk about this? There are mean people in the world. Guys like that don't care how nice you are." Jones wiped down the handle of the pistol with the hem of his T-shirt and dropped the weapon onto the gunman's chest. Scratching behind the husky's ears, he headed for the incline to get the hell out of there. "Though I've gotta say, your distraction was on point."

Jones pressed his palm into his ringing ear. It wasn't so much the noise that bothered him. It was the percussion. He'd bounced back before when a gun had gone off next to his head. This time shouldn't be any different, but he'd check in with Dr. Piel when he got back to headquarters.

He hiked the incline to the spot he'd left the woman he'd pulled from the interrogation room. Only she wasn't there. Jones scanned the terrain, coming up empty. She couldn't have just walked out of there on her own. He'd known men overseas who wouldn't have been able to string together a sentence with the injuries she'd sustained. "I wasn't gone that long, right?"

Gotham yipped as though to answer.

A pair of headlights burst into life a hundred yards past the barbed fence. From his SUV. The beams cut across him a split second before they redirected around. Jones shaded his eyes with one hand and pulled his cell from his cargo pants pocket with the other. Seemed Ms. Caddel hadn't been unconscious, after all. Clever. Then again, it made sense. A woman in her position couldn't be sure of anything after going through what she had. Trusting the man who'd pulled her out of that torture chamber most assuredly didn't come easy.

Jones called into headquarters and lifted the phone to his good ear as the first ring trilled. Then started jogging to catch up with the SUV. "That's what I get for leaving the keys in the ignition."

Chapter Two

She wasn't even sure if she was headed in the right direction.

It was hard to see through the swelling in her right eye, and even then, driving at night had always been dicey. Maggie tightened her aching hands on the steering wheel. The split over her middle knuckle protested with the change in grip, but it felt as though the SUV would rock backward from the uneven landscape at this speed.

Maggie checked the rearview mirror. Dirt kicked up in the back window. She couldn't see anything. That didn't matter. She'd escaped. She'd survived against the odds. She didn't know how. Licking at dry lips, she directed her attention out the windshield. Served the cartel right for keeping the keys in the vehicle. She only hoped there wasn't some kind of locater device they could use to track her down. Because this wasn't over. El Capitan wouldn't stop until she took his secret to her grave.

"You can ditch the car when you get back to the city." Verbally guiding herself through overwhelming to-do lists had always helped. Though some pep talks didn't work as well as others, so she had to act logically. "Okay. A plan. You need a plan. You can't go back to the apartment. Can't use your cards or phone. Don't make this easy for them."

She had to get a hold of Bodhi. Her editor at *American Military News* would know what to do, who to contact. How to get the story out. She could tell him where she'd hidden the photos of the ambush. Once they went public, the cartel wouldn't have any reason to keep coming after her. They'd be trying to cover their own asses. "It's a start."

If the cartel had left the keys in the ignition, maybe they'd left a phone, too. She kept her attention on the minimal spread of landscape ahead and searched for the latch on the middle console. The lid popped back on its hinges, but from what she could feel with one hand, there was nothing but a pistol and a plastic baggie of something that smelled like death.

The gun would at least come in handy, though she'd never handled one in her life.

Maggie blinked through the burn of tears. Endless days of torture should've left her dehydrated, but it seemed she still had a bit left to give. Flashes of pain, of not being able to breathe, of the feeling her stomach was eating itself echoed through her. Swiping at her face, she straightened as dim lighting peppered through the lower corner of the windshield.

What was that? A town? For as much as fourth grade geography taught her about her home state, she didn't have a clue as to what was out here in the middle of the desert. "Pull it together, Caddel. You're not out of the woods yet."

Heading straight for the nearest town was a rookie

move. But the promise of food, water, a change of clothes and maybe a shower gutted her from the inside. Hotels would be the first place El Capitan and his merry band of assholes would look when they realized she wasn't dead.

Why wasn't she dead?

She let the question dissipate as she angled the SUV toward the lights. A road would appear sooner or later. Right? The town—she didn't know its name—seemed to sit between two large walls of cliffs. Protected from outsiders. Given the amount of lights, there couldn't be more than a few hundred residents. There was a chance one of them would take pity on her. "In and out. Get what you need and push through."

The interior of the SUV went dark.

Maggie pried her clammy grip from the steering wheel, pushing herself back into the driver's seat as the engine cut out. She was slowing down. The accelerator wasn't responding. "What? No. No, no, no. Don't do this to me. Please don't do this to me."

The SUV rolled to a stop then inched backward. She shoved her foot onto the brake. The headlights flickered before dying completely. Surrounded by darkness, she couldn't see anything other than the few lights of the town ahead. At least a mile away.

Maggie twisted the key in the ignition, but there was only a rhythmic click. She didn't understand. There'd been at least a half tank of gas according to the meter on the dashboard. Panic launched up her throat, hot as acid and just as suffocating. She couldn't stay here. She had to keep moving. Had to stay a step ahead of the cartel.

Fumbling for the door handle, she tried to shoulder out of the vehicle. But the lock wouldn't disengage. She pulled at the latch, immediately thwarted as the vehicle locked her back in.

Understanding hit. She hadn't run out of gas. The car had been killed remotely. Maggie climbed free from the driver's seat, launching herself to the passenger side. The door wouldn't open. She climbed over the console and into the second row of seats, but neither of the doors nor the cargo hatch would release. Slamming her hand against the glass, she felt as though the walls were closing in. "Let me out!"

She was trapped. A sitting duck. Waiting for the slaughter. El Capitan must've learned she'd escaped. Must've figured out she'd taken one of his vehicles and killed the engine before she had a chance to disappear. Desperate men did desperate things. "Okay. You can do this."

Maggie forced herself to take a deep breath. Pressing her palm into the warm glass, she closed her eyes. The door locks might serve whatever master command had been installed to keep her here, but the windows wouldn't. Interior carpeting caught on the healing skin of one knee as she felt for something—anything—she could use to break through the glass.

"There's nothing here." This didn't make sense. Not even a tire iron or emergency kit? Every car she'd ever bought had come with a spare and a jack. *Sangre por Sangre* was one of the most dangerous drug cartels in the entire country. They smuggled thousands of kilos of drugs across borders and avoided police detection.

It was their job to figure out every nook and cranny in a vehicle and use it to its best potential. Hiding spaces. There had to be… Her fingers fit into a crack between the vehicle's frame and the seemingly solid floor. There.

Climbing back into the second row of seats, she pulled up the cargo cover she'd knelt on. "Holy hell." An entire arsenal of weapons gleamed in the muted moonlight cutting through the back window. "That should work."

Maggie grabbed what looked like a shotgun and let the cargo cover fall back into place. Okay. It was already loaded. All she had to do was point it at the window and pull the trigger, right? Simple enough. She braced the butt of the gun against her shoulder and slipped her finger over the trigger.

A knock punctured the silence. "I believe you have something of mine."

Her finger squeezed the trigger, and the gun hit back into her shoulder. The pain knocked the air from her lungs, and Maggie collapsed onto the center console between the front seats. Something burnt and acidic charged deep into her lungs as it filled the SUV's interior. She tried to cough it up, but the fumes were too heavy. Her heart threatened to beat out of her chest as she gulped for oxygen. She cleared her head enough to see that the shotgun hadn't broken through the glass.

"Yeah. You should know that's reinforced bullet-proof glass. It's going to take a lot more to get through it than a single shot." Movement registered from the driver's side of the vehicle. "I'm going to unlock the doors, all right? I'd appreciate it if you didn't shoot me."

"Come any closer and I will." That voice. She'd

heard it before. Maggie scrambled to match it with the catalog she'd made over the course of the past few days in hell, but it wasn't fitting. Her nervous system had reached its all-time panic mode. She couldn't go back. She couldn't take another round of interrogation. She had to get out of here. By any means necessary. Sweat beaded in her hairline and made her bloody, tattered clothes feel too tight. "Just stay back. Let me think."

There was nowhere for her to go. The SUV wouldn't start. The doors wouldn't let her out. She couldn't even count on the guns to get her out of this mess.

"Your name is Caddel, right? Maggie Caddel?" He seemed to be keeping his distance, though Maggie couldn't pinpoint his location with all the chaos fluttering through her head. No accent. Not like the others. American born. "You're a war correspondent for *American Military News.* You've been reporting on the *Sangre por Sangre* cartel for the past year."

"Knowing my name doesn't give you the right to execute me." She set aside the shotgun and righted herself. The second he unlocked the doors from his side, she would bolt out the other door. She might not be able to outrun him, but at least then she'd have a chance of dying on her own terms.

"Does this look like a face that wants to execute you?" The man's outline thickened through the window a split second before something else took its place.

Maggie stared at the face of a dog through the tinted window. A husky from the look of him. Full grown. His white hair stood out in the growing moonlight. He wriggled to get free of the strong hands holding him midair, nipping at exposed skin. That song, the one kids sang about buying a doggy in the window, came to mind. Okay. She was losing her mind. "Is that a dog?"

Her brain was playing tricks on her. That was the only explanation for a husky to be out here in the middle of the desert.

"His name's Gotham. You might not remember, but we're the ones who pulled you out of that interrogation room back at the cartel's headquarters." His voice wormed into the deepest recesses of her mind. *I'm going to get you out of here.* Not one of her captors. "You know, before you stole my vehicle and left me for dead."

Her skin felt too tight, her bones too big for her body. Maggie didn't know what to do, what to think. This was all…impossible.

"If you promise not to shoot me when I unlock the doors, I'll let you pet him. He's soft. I just gave him a bath this morning," he said.

What other choice did she have? She wasn't getting out of here without his help, and there was no way she could outrun anyone at this point. She couldn't deny the idea of petting a dog after what she'd been through wasn't everything she needed right then either. Exhaustion embedded deep into the fibers of her muscles, and her hand fell away from the shotgun. "Fine. If you unlock the doors, I promise not to shoot you."

JONES LET GOTHAM down and raised his cell back to his ear. He didn't know what waited on the other side of that fractured glass, but one thing was for certain: he wasn't going to let the cartel catch up to the woman he'd extracted. "Go ahead and unlock the doors, Scarlett."

The SUV's doors released with the touch of a button from Socorro's security consultant. Just as she'd killed the vehicle's engine. Scarlett Beam was a new addition to the team, but one that came in handy more often than not. "Need backup?"

"No." Undeserved confidence slid through him. "I've got it from here. Thanks."

Ending the call, he pocketed his phone, then reached for the back seat door on the driver's side.

The door flew open without him touching the handle, and Maggie Caddel lunged free. It took a lot of visible effort for her to stay on her feet, but Jones gave her room as her nervous system adapted. Her shoulders and chest worked to get as much oxygen as possible. Hell, she was in a bad state. It was a wonder she still had any life in her after what'd happened. She flicked her tongue over busted lips. "You said I could pet your dog."

"He likes it when you put your face next to his." He motioned to Gotham without invading her personal space. Suffering through what she had, she didn't need him imposing himself on her. She needed to feel safe.

Crouching, Maggie scratched bruised and cut fingers into the K9's fluffy coat as Jones had done hundreds of times in the short weeks they'd been together. Then she set her face against Gotham's. The husky pressed his face into hers, and they closed their eyes as one, enjoying the feel of one another. The sight was almost enough to ease Jones's defenses. How would he have convinced her to leave the SUV if he hadn't been dragging a husky through the desert?

"You're with Socorro, aren't you? That military contractor the Pentagon sent to dismantle *Sangre por Sangre*. I've read about you and your team. You're the combat controller from the air force. Driscoll, right?"

"At your service." Jones hiked his thumbs into his cargo pants pockets. The way she said his name... It wasn't anything special. She'd read it on a roster that belonged to his employer, but there'd been a bit of a catch on the last syllable that stuck with him. He dared a step closer as Maggie shifted—unbalanced—on her feet. She was running on fumes, and adrenaline could only take a person so far. Knowing the cartel, she'd been deprived of food, water, probably sleep. Any one of those came with disastrous effects, but all of them together? She was on the verge of collapse. "But considering you stole my vehicle, I think we're past the point of formalities. You can call me Jones."

"I didn't know it was yours." Maggie pried Gotham from her face, seemingly coming to terms with the events of the night. Her eyes, even in the dim light of the moon, were losing focus. "They were going to kill me. I just... I needed to get out of there."

"You don't ever have to apologize to me for trying to survive." Jones took that last step, grabbing for Maggie as her legs gave out. "It's okay. I've got you."

"I'm tired." She was slurring her words. Not a good sign.

"I know. We'll get you fixed up." Jones whistled for Gotham to follow as he worked to get Maggie into the vehicle. Hauling her into his side, he guided her across the back seat of the SUV. The shotgun she'd tried using to blast her way out through the back window lay across the floor. He had to hand it to her. She was mighty resourceful. Though, in her line of work, he imagined she had to be to stay out of trouble. Guess that resourcefulness hadn't been enough this time around. He let Gotham cuddle into Maggie's side. "Keep her company, would you?"

Because there was a chance she'd wake up panicked, not knowing where she was. Who she was. He'd seen it once before. The terror that came with imprisonment and torture. It wasn't anything he wished on his worst enemy. Jones slid behind the wheel and started the SUV. The engine growled to life. The headlights cut across the uneven landscape as he maneuvered toward home base.

Jones set Maggie in his sights through the rearview mirror. Hell. He should've gotten into the cartel headquarters sooner. He should've realized the reason Sosimo Toledano hadn't ventured out for the past three days. The son of a bitch had been in the middle of breaking Maggie down physically, mentally, emotionally. But why? What could a war correspondent for a failing military news magazine possibly have to do with *Sangre por Sangre*? "What did you get yourself into?"

He hadn't expected an answer.

"I saw them." Maggie turned onto her back, her voice distant, not entirely solid. "They killed…everyone."

Killed everyone? "Who did they kill, Maggie?"

She didn't respond this time. Her body would direct its energy to her major organs before it started shutting down. Heart, brain, lungs.

She needed help. Now.

Jones floored the accelerator as he fishtailed onto the single lane dirt road headed straight into the south side of the valley. As cartels battled over territory and attempted to upend law enforcement and government throughout New Mexico, organizations like Socorro Security were key in neutralizing the threat to the surrounding towns, but something had changed over the past few months. *Sangre por Sangre* wasn't just intensifying their assaults on the general public as they had in the past. They were strategizing. Hitting specific targets. Moving more product. Trafficking more innocent lives. Recruiting heavier than ever before.

And Maggie had somehow ended up in the middle of it.

Gotham's whine cut through the interior of the SUV.

"Hang on. We're almost there." A branch of dirt road split off from the main road, and Jones took it without hesitation. A spotlight lit up ahead. In the dead of night, it looked out of place surrounded by thousand-foot cliffs and bare desert, but once the sun came up, a gleaming modern structure of tinted glass and steel would peek out from the mountainside.

Jones followed the lesser-worn path as fast as he dared without dislodging Maggie from the back seat. The front of the SUV dipped as he lined up with the garage entrance. Scarlett had upgraded security to the point he didn't have to swipe his badge. The tracking node she'd implanted in his forearm was enough to get him through the gate as long as his heart was still beating.

He swung the SUV in front of the sleek elevator doors leading into the heart of headquarters and shoved the vehicle into Park. Shouldering out of the car, Jones raced for the keypad installed in the wall, and hit the emergency medical button. "Doc, I need you in the parking garage."

He didn't bother waiting for an answer as he rounded to the back passenger side door. Overhead lights reflected in Maggie's heavy eyes. Gotham refused to budge as Jones threaded his arms under hers and pulled her free from the SUV. Time seemed to freeze. Where the hell was the doc? "Help is coming, Maggie. Stay with me."

"Find them," she said. "You have to find them. Everyone deserves...to know the truth."

"Don't worry about that right now." Confusion wasn't enough to hold him back from getting her help, but Gotham didn't seem to want to let Maggie go. He planted his front paws on her legs as though he'd claimed her as his own. "Why do you have to make everything so much harder than it needs to be?"

The elevator pinged with its arrival. A flood of organized chaos exploded from within as two women breached the garage.

Dr. Nafessa Piel wasn't the type of on-call stitcher to wear one of those white lab coats unless she expected a lot of blood. Socorro's doc pulled her hair back in a tie and shoved her long sleeves over her elbows as she approached the back seat. "Tell me everything I need to know."

Socorro's security operative Scarlett Beam stood back, letting the doctor work.

"I found her." An unfamiliar loyalty urged Jones to keep his hands on Maggie as the doc tried to wedge him out of the way—to comfort, to console, he didn't know—but every second he kept Dr. Piel from doing her job was another second that could put the journalist in danger. "Cartel worked her up pretty good. I don't know how long. Couple days, maybe. She was conscious until a minute ago. Talking, even."

Dr. Piel pulled a flashlight and peeled Maggie's right eye open, shining the light in directly. "Her pupils aren't dilating. She's suffered some kind of head trauma. Possibly swelling. We can't move her without supporting her neck and head. Scarlett, get the dog out of here. Jones, get one of the guys down here. I'm going to need all the help I can get."

Scarlett dragged Gotham free of Maggie's lap and latched onto his collar. His whine punctured through the vehicle, as though the husky couldn't bear to be separated from his new friend. Jones didn't have the voice to tell his partner he knew exactly what that felt like. "Come on, rookie. Your dad's gotta work. Let's see what Hans and Gruber are doing upstairs," she said, referring to her two Dobermans.

Jones's head pounded in rhythm to his racing heart as he sent out the SOS. In less than a minute, Cash Meyers—Socorro's forward observer—hit the parking garage with portable backboard in hand. "What do you need?"

"I've got her head. Jones, you're in the middle. Cash, get her feet. We move as one. Understand?" The authority in the doc's voice would cut through rock. "There's no telling what kind of internal damage she's suffered. Any jostling could make her injuries worse."

Jones took his position, squeezing his too-large body between the back passenger door and Maggie's slim frame. He threaded his hands beneath her hips. And froze. Her underside was wet. Warm. Extracting his hand, he tried to breathe through the metallic-sweet odor hitting his senses. Blood. A lot of it. "Doc, I think we've made it worse."

"Move," Dr. Piel said. "Now!"

Chapter Three

She should've stayed in Albuquerque.

Maggie tried to crane her neck to one side, but something hard and itchy kept her in place. A groan escaped up her throat as a deep ache drilled through her. She was back in her cell. The one that leaked from the exposed pipe overhead. Coming around from another round of interrogation. El Capitan hadn't killed her yet. Which meant she hadn't given him what he wanted. Good. She'd hold out as long as she could.

A lightness took hold in her legs, in her back and hips. There wasn't really any pain there. She just felt... immobile. Maggie tried to curl her fingers into her palms. Pressure, not pinching. A tear burned in her left eye. She could still feel sensation. Not a spinal injury. Strapped to a chair? No. That wasn't it, either. Her hands were free. Though letting her captors know she was conscious hadn't worked out for her before, she cracked her eyelids.

Not darkness as she expected. Dim lighting—calming, warm, with a slight airy feeling—highlighted some kind of hospital room. Blackout curtains framed an entire wall of tinted glass to one side. It was dark on the other side.

Though middle of the night or engineered that way, she didn't know. Maggie memorized what she could of the room in the glass's reflection.

Including the man seated on the opposite side of her bed.

Familiarity seeped into the tension that came so automatically these days. That face. She knew that face. Worn, battle-hardened in a way she'd seen in so many soldiers, but at the same time handsome. Thick, groomed facial hair tried to hide the shape of his jaw. She'd felt it. When he'd held her against his chest. Her forehead had brushed against it. Soft. Softer than she'd expected. It'd been that single second of sensory input that'd kept her from spiraling through the fear. Which, now, seemed ridiculous. She'd been abducted, questioned and tortured for days that had now blurred together. And this man's facial hair was the only thing that kept her from falling apart at the very end. "Do you know how beautiful you are?"

The operative at her bedside leaned into her peripheral vision. The lines around his eyes had shallowed, and suddenly he seemed years younger. His mouth quirked to one side and accentuated the slight hood over his light eyes. "Doc said she gave you something for the pain. Though it seems she might've dosed you a bit too much."

Embarrassment heated through her. The lightness in her legs and hips. No wonder she couldn't make sense of her own thoughts. "Where am I?"

"Socorro. Try to take it easy. You've been through a lot, but you're safe here." A transformation took place in a matter of milliseconds. Where there'd been almost a kind of relief in his expression, there was a guardedness now. As though he'd already said too much. "You remember me?"

"You locked me in your SUV." Her throat burned with a dryness she'd become used to, but it felt so overwhelming now. Out of place.

His laugh rumbled deep through him. Not of its own accord but dampened. Controlled. The way he ducked his head down to avoid exposure for that break in composure said a lot, too. This was a man constantly on the defense. Always looking for the next threat and calculating how to neutralize it. "Yeah. I might be a little protective of my stuff."

Splinters of memory returned. Not all at once, but almost like an out-of-order slideshow she'd never want to sit through. Her being dragged from the interrogation room. Him catching her as she ran through every scenario of escape in the middle of the desert. And…a dog. Her neck itched. Maggie raised one hand to her throat, hitting something solid and plastic protecting her from collarbone to chin. Air evaporated from her chest. This…this was a neck brace. She clawed at it. Bandages around her hands kept her from getting a good grip on the edge. "What… What is this? What happened?"

Jones shot to his feet, closing the distance between them. "It's okay. Dr. Piel wanted to make sure you wouldn't aggravate any swelling in your neck or head while she was going through your bloodwork and scans. It's precautionary after what you've been through."

"Swelling?" She tried to sit up.

"You took quite a beating, Maggie. You're lucky to be alive." Calloused hands slid around hers to pry her fingernails from between the hard plastic and her jawline. The contact was warm and slow, but her nervous system wasn't convinced of his promise of safety.

"What did they do?" She couldn't hide the desperation sliding into her voice. This wasn't part of the plan. She'd started over. She'd made something of herself. On her own. Despite the lack of support from her family, friends and everyone else who'd turned their backs on her, she'd overcome it all. She couldn't take a step back. Not now. "What's wrong with me?"

A sadness that had no right to warp Jones's face cut through her. "You lost a lot of blood. Luckily the doc keeps a few bags of every blood type on hand in case one of us does something stupid. You needed a transfusion, and you sustained quite of bit of bruising and cuts over your whole body. There are a couple of minor rib fractures, but the worst is in your back. Dr. Piel called it a spinal cord hemorrhage."

"I don't... I don't understand." Maggie closed her eyes against the onslaught of memories coming now. Every strike. Every question. Every slice of pain.

Jones moved into her full line of sight. Slowly, strategic. Like he was approaching some kind of wounded animal he didn't want to frighten, but it was all done in vain. There wasn't anything that was going to make this okay. "You started bleeding on the way here. I didn't realize it until we were getting you out of the SUV. Dr. Piel found a puncture wound in your spinal column once we got you on the table. You've been losing small amounts of spinal fluid. Let me get her. She can explain it better than I can."

Maggie clutched his hand, digging her broken fingernails in deeper than necessary.

"Are you saying…" She was trying to wrap her head around each and every one of his words. Trying to make them make sense, but a thickness of pain medication and sleeplessness and hunger and thirst seemed to be battling against her. There was only one that stood out among the others. One that would rip this new life she'd made for herself away. "Am I going to be paralyzed? Can I walk?"

"Yeah, Maggie. You can walk, but it's going to take time. It's going to hurt, and you're going to need a lot of help with recovery over the next few weeks." His voice softened. The sound of pity. "Dr. Piel has already called in the best physician who has experience with this type of injury. You'll be back on your feet before you know it."

This type of injury. A downward pull started in her gut and pinned her to the bed. Time. Pain. Help. No. She'd already suffered through what she'd hoped had been the biggest hill in her life. She couldn't do this again. She couldn't let herself be that victim all over again. Maggie tried to kick at the too-soft sheets and heavy comforter to get free of the cage they'd created, but the prickling in her feet intensified to the point of hot coals. "No. I can't. I can't stay here."

"I know what you're going through." Jones backed up to give her space, but it wasn't enough. "I know you feel trapped, Maggie. I know this feels impossible, but if you try to leave, you're just going to hurt yourself more."

The walls were closing in, and Maggie didn't have the discipline not to let her brain's mind games get to her this time. Exhaustion broke barriers faster than anything else she'd gone through. If it hadn't been for Jones pulling her out of that interrogation room, she would've given in to El Capitan. She would've told that son of a bitch anything he'd wanted to know if he'd promised to just let her sleep. She clutched the bedrail to heft herself up. The neck brace cut into the underside of her jaw. The added sensation gave her mind something tangible to grab onto, and she wasn't letting go. She pulled her legs over the side of the bed with her free hand. Hell, she'd been turned into a mummy. So many bandages. So many injuries. How had she survived? "You don't know. You don't know…what I've been through, and I hope you never will."

He was suddenly there, right in her line of escape. Massive hands locked onto the bed on either side of her. A blockade of muscle and determination and authority, but Maggie's gut said he hadn't gone through the trouble of pulling her out of the cartel's lair to keep her captive. He'd move if pushed. Because that was the kind of man he was. Loyal but not dominating. "Yes, I do, and I give you my word it will get better, but you've got to put in the work, and you've got to let me help you."

Something hot stabbed through her. A sincerity in his words that made her want to believe he actually understood her mindset. That he understood her body wanted nothing but to die, but her spirit refused to give up and that she couldn't just sit here. No judgment in his voice. No room for excuses. This man—whoever he was and wherever he'd come from—believed she was safe. She could practically feel the heat coming off of him. Something she thought she'd never feel again, and Maggie wanted nothing more than to lean into that heat. To feel support from someone else so she could just take a couple minutes to breathe. "You don't understand. I can't stay here. They'll never stop. He'll never stop, and the longer I stay here, the more danger everyone is in."

Jones pried his hands from the mattress on either side of her, and she found herself missing the clarity of soap and man in an instant. "The men who took you." It was as though he could see right through her. That he knew her. "*Sangre por Sangre* doesn't take prisoners. Not unless you have something they want. So what do they want with you, Maggie Caddel?"

The pressure of holding back these past few days— or however long it'd been since that night in the desert —crushed her from the inside. "I wasn't supposed to be there, but I saw everything. The man who interrogated me. He killed them all. And I have the proof."

HER HANDS SHOOK, drawing Jones closer.

A simple flick of her tongue across those busted lips was enough to get his full attention. He should've gone after Sosimo Toledano. Given the bastard a taste of his own medicine for doing what he'd done to Maggie. But the choice to save her life or complete his mission hadn't been easy in the moment. Dredging those memories up wasn't going to do her a damn bit of good either. Her recovery. Her healing. That was all Jones could focus on right now. The cracks in his hands caught on the cuts and scrapes in hers against the mattress. "Tell me what happened, Maggie."

"It was stupid." Her voice lost the command he'd admired in the desert. Right after she'd pumped a round of shotgun shells into his back window and threatened to shoot him, and he couldn't help but hold her hand tighter. "I've been following *Sangre por Sangre* members for just under a year to try to get my first story. Low-level dealers to start with, but every once in a while, they'd break off from their routines and lead me to someone higher up the chain. I thought if I waited long enough, if I could uncover the man at the top, that would give me something to secure my future."

"You've been following drug cartel members, alone." The words almost didn't seem real. Socorro had people like him—trained in reconnaissance and combat, soldiers who knew what to look for and how to respond to a threat—to cover organizations like *Sangre por Sangre* and report back to the Pentagon. And she'd walked into the hornet's nest without so much as a second thought?

"You don't understand. I'm the newest war correspondent at the magazine. I don't have as much experience as the others." Maggie swiped at her face. The exhaustion wasn't hollowing her eyes as much now, but the bruising around her temples and cheeks had darkened significantly. "This job... I need it to work, and all the big stories were going to the veteran journalists. Bodhi—my editor—hasn't liked any of my submissions so far. He was going to let me go if I didn't produce a story worth printing. I needed something."

A suction of gravity triggered in his chest. Jones retracted his hand as that invisible force threatened to rip him into a million pieces. Shoving himself upright, he circled the room to try to walk it off, but there was no point. She'd risked this one precious life for the chance of landing a story. "And you really believe a job is more important than your life?"

"You don't know me." Her accusation didn't come with anger. Mere observation pulled him up short from raging around the hospital room, trying to make her see the absolute ridiculousness of her motives. "You pulled me out of that interrogation room, or whatever it was, and I appreciate it. You saved my life, but that doesn't give you the right to berate me for my choices."

Hell. She was right. They weren't friends. They were barely acquaintances. Jones scrubbed his hand down his face, hoping to take the heat burning in his veins with it. Didn't help. The best thing he could do was focus on the facts. On how she'd ended up in *Sangre por Sangre*'s grasp and why they hadn't killed her. "All right. So you started following low-level members. How does that get you under the fist of one of the most wanted lieutenants on our radar?"

"Two weeks ago, one of the soldiers I'd been following was pulled off his corner. Then I noticed others. *Sangre por Sangre*'s income depends on those corners in Albuquerque and other cities like it. I thought something had happened, but the longer I watched, the more I realized they were being recruited within the cartel. Under a single lieutenant."

"Sosimo Toledano," he said.

"I only knew him as El Capitan. That's what the others called him between…" She gestured to the length of her body. "I got the impression Toledano was organizing a coup against the old leadership. A story like that would blow my editor's mind and shoot me to the top of the roster for my next assignment. I couldn't pass up the opportunity, so I started watching him. The more I watched, the more I learned. Turns out your Sosimo Toledano is the son of the man at the top of *Sangre por Sangre*. The Pentagon has been looking for him for months in connection with a series of attacks throughout New Mexico. Executions, even raids going on in the smaller towns. One as recent as last week."

"Socorro is well versed in Toledano's profile." Because of him. Because Jones had been assigned to put the pieces together. Though he hadn't expected Maggie to be one of the missing pieces.

"A few days ago—I couldn't tell you how many— I followed him and the members he'd recruited. They drove out to the middle of the desert. I stayed back as far as I could with my headlights off. Then I heard the first gunshot. It was hard to see, so I got out and jogged to get a better view. I had my camera." She shook her head in some kind of attempt to undo the past. "And I walked… I walked right into an ambush."

Every cell in Jones's body hiked to attention. There hadn't been reports of an ambush against the cartel. It certainly hadn't come from Socorro. "What kind of ambush?"

"The kind where a cartel lieutenant kills ten American soldiers and buries the evidence without anybody knowing," she said.

Jones lost the air in his lungs. That…wasn't possible. There were any number of contingencies built into an operation like this. Backup teams, strategy, superiors who'd left the fieldwork to guys like him. If she was telling the truth, someone had to know what the hell had happened out there in the middle of that desert. The weight couldn't just fall to Maggie. "You got photos."

"I hid as soon as I realized what was happening, turned off the flash on my camera and just started shooting. They had no idea I was there." A shudder ran through her from neck to hips. "But once the bodies were buried, I knew I had to get out of there. I started running for my car, but it was so dark, I tripped over a rock. My camera broke, but I managed to save the SD card. I shoved it into a crack in the dirt where I fell. One of the cartel's soldiers must've heard me fall. He found me. I fought him off as long as I could."

The adrenaline rush of realizing she'd risked her life for the chance of writing the next military headline waned. "But the SD card with all the photos you took is still out there."

"That's what El Capitan wanted. My camera, but the SD card was gone. He knows I hid it." Tears glittered in her eyes. Knuckles tight around the hem of her sheets, Maggie refused to look at him. "He was going to kill me. The things he did…" She shut her eyes against the abhorrent images Jones had no doubt would haunt her for the rest of her life. "Nobody should be able to live through that."

"But you did." Pressure stuck behind his sternum. He'd been here before. At the side of a hospital bed just like this one, trying to come up with something significant and comforting to say. Holding another hand that'd been broken during the course of interrogation. Jones memorized the damage done to the smooth skin along the back of Maggie's hand. Just as he'd done all those years ago while he'd given consent to have his brother taken off life support. Only this time was different. This time, he could fix it. He could do something. "You survived. Despite the odds. That means something."

"That I'm too stubborn for my own good?" A scoff escaped her limited control. The break in her composure was only temporary, because behind the sarcasm was a wounded and badly beaten soul. "My parents always warned me my pigheadedness would get me into trouble. I thought they'd just meant what would happen if I left my ex. I didn't think it'd land me in the center of the cartel's cross hairs."

Jones didn't really know what that felt like. The whole parent thing. Not in any stable sense of the word, at least. That was what happened when you were moved from foster home to foster home. Some good, some bad. No attachment to any given place or the people in it. Attachment led to emotion. Emotion led to weakness. Weakness led to mistakes. And he wasn't about to make the same mistake as he had with his brother.

"All you have to worry about is getting better, Maggie. The photos, Sosimo Toledano, your job. None of that matters. Understand?"

"He won't stop. You know that, right? Toledano isn't going to stop hunting me. He'll come here." Maggie's eyes fluttered with exhaustion, casting dark eyelashes across the tops of her cheeks. They fanned out in a way that should only be possible through the gravity-defying technology of makeup, yet Jones couldn't find a trace of it on her face. Her chin deviated from its center position over her chest as she seemed to relax into the bed against her will. "And he'll hurt anyone who gets in his way."

"I'm not going to let that happen. I give you my word." He couldn't seem to let go of her hand, even as she drifted into unconsciousness. The painkillers were doing their job, but it would take a whole lot more than a combination of drugs to put Maggie back on her feet.

And he was going to be there. Whatever it took. Because she didn't deserve this. *Sangre por Sangre* had crossed a line, and Jones was going to be the one to make them pay for overstepping. Once and for all.

Convincing his nervous system he didn't have to hold on to her took longer than it should have. He could still feel her hand in his as he extracted himself from her hospital room and headed down the black corridor toward Ivy Bardot's office. Socorro Security had been contracted to dismantle the *Sangre por Sangre* cartel by any means necessary, but up until this point, everything he and the team had done had been reactionary.

Now was the time for them to make their move.

Chapter Four

The pain shot down the back of her thigh. Not as bad as the last time she'd pried herself out of bed. The need to get on her feet, to keep moving, tightened in her chest to the point she couldn't breathe beneath the soft, light sheets. Her stomach battled against the familiar taste of full-course breakfasts, lunches and dinners—with desserts—over the past three days.

She couldn't take it anymore.

Being taken care of. She couldn't sit here and wait for El Capitan and his men to finish what they'd started. Sosimo Toledano. That was his name, but knowing it didn't make any of this better. She'd given Socorro—given Jones—enough time and enough information to take what'd happened and construct their own narrative for action. She'd done her job. Now it was time to get back to her life. While she still could.

Maggie pressed her feet into the cold, black tile. This whole place looked as though it'd been taken directly out of a science fiction movie. Big windows stared out over the desert landscape—tinted, most likely bullet-proof—and when it got dark, there was nothing but stars and distant lights on the other side of the glass.

Alpine Valley. That was the little town she'd tried to run to the other night. Small, out of the way, isolated. It looked like any other town right now, but the people there had found themselves at the mercy of *Sangre por Sangre* and a bombing that led to a massive landslide that buried two hundred homes in the past two months. It'd been all over the news at the time. There was something to be said of that kind of strength. Of a community as underprotected and vulnerable as that one coming together against a threat.

She could hide there if she kept her head down. Not forever. Just long enough to secure a phone, maybe a car. The cartel would catch on if she stayed in one place too long, but it was a start. She was fairly certain she could locate the site of the ambush to collect the SD card she'd hidden. El Capitan had taken her wallet, phone, even her allergy meds. She'd lived with less. She could do it again.

Maggie stripped free of the gown that gave Dr. Piel access to her spine. The bleeding in her back had stopped two days ago, but there was still a bit of swelling around the puncture wound and an intense headache she couldn't get rid of. She'd told Jones the truth. She couldn't remember being injected with drugs or hallucinogens, but whatever Toledano had set out to do had failed. She wasn't going to give him a second chance.

Cold air constricted her skin as she grabbed for the packaged scrubs, a top and bottom set on the side table. She threaded her feet into the bottoms, forced to move slower than she wanted to go as the muscles around her

spine stretched and released. The top went on easier.
The socks took longer than both put together, but within
minutes, she was dressed. No sign of a pair of shoes.
Guess those weren't considered necessary for recovery.
Or the people here were trying to keep her from leaving.

Her left foot dragged slightly behind the right as
she headed for the door. The heavy metal took more
energy than she expected to wedge open. There were
no phones ringing off the hook, no PA announcements
overhead. No nurses and doctors rushing with crash
carts or responding to patients. Everything was quiet.
Empty. Only the slight pound of her pulse behind her
ears told her she hadn't suffered permanent hearing
damage from the high-frequency noise her abductors
had forced her to listen to for hours at a time.

She dared a step into the monochromatic hallways.
Black everywhere. The ceilings, the floors, the walls,
the artwork. There was nowhere to hide in a place like
this. Pressure grew in her chest, and she looked up to
see a single camera staring back at her from the space
where the wall met the ceiling. No light to indicate
whether it was recording or not, but this was a security company. Why else have it installed?

Maggie ducked under the device and pulled out the
single wire connecting it to the metal frame below the
lens. "You're going to have to work harder than that
to keep me here."

This place was a maze. Every turn led to another
corridor, another conference room, another door secured with a keypad. Disconnecting every camera as
she went along, she had the distinct impression that

somewhere in here the members of Socorro were just waiting to see how far she'd make it before she gave up and went back to her room. But she'd never quit anything in her life. She wasn't about to start now.

She had to get out of here. She had to get the SD card she'd buried and contact Bodhi. It was the only way to stop the cartel from coming after her for the rest of her life. Maggie turned into a dead end. "You've got to be kidding me."

A yip registered from behind.

She spun around, confronting the husky she'd met while trying to escape the cartel in a bulletproof SUV. The night she'd been brought here. He settled his furry butt on the floor, staring up at her with a whole wide world of innocence in his face.

"I remember you. Gotham, right?" Maggie dared a step toward him, hand extended to pet him, then froze. Did Socorro let their K9s roam the halls of their own free will? Or did this mean Jones was close by? She didn't have time to find out.

"Do you know how to get out of here?" Did she really expect a dog to understand her? Military K9s were intelligent, disciplined even. But that didn't make them capable of the English language. "Um, out?"

Gotham cocked his head to one side a split second before he padded dead ahead, nails clicking against the floors. She'd take that as a good sign. Maggie struggled to keep up with him. Even as steady as he was, he was much faster than her injuries allowed her. Another streak of pain shot down her left leg, bringing her to a stop as Gotham took a turn ahead. "Wait!"

She grabbed onto the back of her leg, willing it to move, but the pain was too much. Like a nerve had been pinched all along her left side. She'd never catch up to him like this. Which meant she wasn't going to be able to get out of here. Maggie sucked in a deep breath to counter the crushing effect weighing her down as she steadied one hand against the nearest wall. "Baby steps."

That was what her therapist had said. She wasn't supposed to look at the whole puzzle and try to solve it in one go. It hadn't worked in the middle of her divorce, and it wouldn't work now. She had to break it down into pieces. One step forward. Then another. That was all she could focus on. Not the pain. Not the hopelessness. Not anything but the next foot in front of her. Maggie took that first step. Then the second. Her leg threatened to collapse out from under her, but she held strong.

That success was enough to bolster her confidence. Maggie made it to the corner where she'd lost Gotham.

And faced off with the man whose voice she couldn't get out of her head.

"Figured if you wanted to leave this bad, I might as well show you the way." Jones scratched Gotham's ears, and the dog closed his eyes. Traitor.

"You were watching me on the cameras." She didn't have the strength for embarrassment or denial. Every second she wasted here was another second *Sangre por Sangre* got away with what they'd done. Evidence would be contaminated. The bodies would start decomposing, and while she fully believed in the science and technology used to solve murders, the first forty-eight hours of any investigation were crucial. And those were already gone. "I'm not going to apologize. I don't like feeling trapped. Did you at least get the show you expected?"

"All I saw was a woman bent on proving she's the one calling the shots. Well, before you started pulling the power on the cameras. Didn't see much after that, so I sent Gotham to find you. Scarlett isn't too happy, but I can't actually think of a time when she was."

Jones offered her his free hand. Like she had a choice in what she did next, but it was a ruse, wasn't it? Because there was no way he was going to let her walk out of here in her condition, let alone try to take on the cartel single-handedly. "Shall we?"

Maggie visually followed the cracked lines in his palm. Worn, rough, aged. Hands that'd seen a lifetime of violence and anger. And yet so contrary to the easiness in his gaze. It was almost enough to release the tension in her gut. Almost. "Fine, but I get to pet the dog."

Jones's deep laugh rumbled through the corridor as he stepped aside to give her room between him and Gotham. Dipping down to scratch the husky added to the strain on her back and leg, but within an instant, Jones was there. Holding her up. Letting her use him as a crutch without her uttering a word. As though he'd known exactly what she was feeling. How much she hurt. Not just physically. But emotionally. Mentally. He braced his arm at her back but let her lead at her own pace.

"How did Gotham know where to find me?" she asked.

"Don't take this the wrong way, but he's a human remains recovery K9." She could just see how hard it was for him to say that with a straight face.

"Do I really smell that bad?" Maggie tried not to stick her nose in her armpit to gauge how long she'd been without a shower. Any shift could disrupt the delicate balance they'd created these last couple of yards.

"You smell fine." Jones angled her to the left and down another corridor. How he knew where he was going in this maze, she could only guess. "He knows your scent now. Given the opportunity, he could track you down within a mile of your location."

"That's impressive." Maggie fisted her hands in Gotham's fur as she slowed. Despite the need to keep moving, to escape, she'd always been at the mercy of her curiosity. "But that doesn't explain why you sent him after me in the first place. Why you brought me here for medical attention. Why you even pulled me out of that interrogation room. I'm just some random stranger you happened to come across. Why bother?"

"That's easy." Jones kept his arm in place—in case she needed it—but there was some part of her just then that thought maybe he needed the connection, too. "Because I didn't want what happened to my brother to happen to you."

"WHAT DO YOU MEAN?" Maggie held her own as though out to prove she didn't need him. As though she didn't need anyone. It was a self-defense technique. Not one born out of training, but out of necessity. Though a part of him wondered why she was so desperate to convince everyone she could get through this life alone. "What does any of this have to do with your brother?"

Jones hadn't meant to expose that part of his life. Not to her. Not to anyone. Least of all someone he'd just met within the past seventy-two hours. And a journalist, for crying out loud. A burning sensation set up residence behind his sternum. It still hurt. Thinking about what his brother had gone through, how his strength—especially of a man of Kincaide's size and abilities—had dwindled in the end. It'd changed him. Inside and out. And there hadn't been anything Jones could do but watch as the only person who gave a damn about him struggled to survive. Then lost.

"It doesn't matter. My point is I can help you, Maggie. I'm good at what I do. I can protect you from the cartel. I can help you find out what happened the night you were taken and to recover those photos."

Not Socorro. Him. Because while he fully trusted Scarlett and the others to have his back in the field, this was something he had to do. For Kincaide. For the hole left behind in his chest after his brother's death. To give Maggie a reason to keep going. He needed this.

"I've studied *Sangre por Sangre* for close to a year. I've seen what they can do and how little they care for the people they do it to, Jones." The laceration in her lip split as she flinched at some pain he couldn't see. Her right leg was starting to shake under her weight, an indicator she was having problems with her left. "I don't even know you, and I know that I wouldn't wish what happened to me on my worst enemy." Maggie let Gotham slide back to Jones's side. "Thank you for pulling me out of that dark place. And for saving my life. I wouldn't be here without you or your team, and I owe you for that, but I can't let anyone else get trapped in this hell with me."

She used the wall for leverage as she turned her back on him and shuffled along the corridor.

Gotham's whine echoed off the walls.

That all-too-familiar sense of loss cut through him at the thought of her walking out those doors unprotected, injured. Jones barely acknowledged the consequences of his next question, willing to do whatever was required to keep Maggie from taking on an entire drug cartel alone. "Even a source?"

Three words. That was all it took to hook into her personal drive. He was good at that, seeing a person's— most especially a combatant's—deepest compulsion and dragging it out. It was those limited moments in the field that'd given him an advantage over so many others.

Stringy blond hair acted as an effective barrier to her expression as she pulled up short. "Is that an offer?"

"You told me how important your job is as a war correspondent, that you need it." Jones would pay hell for this. Socorro Security operatives signed NDAs once onboarded to the team. Any and all press went through one woman and one woman only: Ivy Bardot, Socorro's founder. He could lose his job for this. Worse, he could lose his team, but he hadn't known what else to do to keep Maggie from leaving.

"Think about it. You'll be the only journalist who has access to this team and our plans against *Sangre por Sangre*, after the fact, of course. That kind of information hasn't been available to any other news outlet before now. You'll be *American Military News*'s star reporter. All those other writers won't have anything on you."

Maggie angled toward him, and hell if it didn't look as though it took everything in her power not to collapse right there in the middle of the floor. The bruising around her face and down her neck shifted colors around the perimeter. More blue-green than black and purple. Her body was doing everything in its power to heal, but the second she left this building, she was putting herself at risk. "Why would you do that?"

"I told you. I can help." He realized the offer must've seemed ridiculous with him standing there with a husky at his side, but Jones had never been so sure of anything in his life than he was about this deal. "If you let me."

Maggie dropped her arm away from the wall. "Becoming a source isn't just about handing over information. It's about mutual trust. I need to know I can rely on you, that the information I'm getting isn't being filtered or rewritten in any way. That what I'm getting is raw and real. That's the only way this can work between us."

"You have my word." No matter what it took to keep it. "But I want the same deal. If we do this, we do this together. All I ask is that you trust me in return. No lies. No filtering. If you're in pain, I want to know you're going to take care of yourself. If you're going after those photos you hid before your abduction, I'm right by your side. Agreed?"

She attempted to cross her arms over her chest, but the effort looked harder than it should've been. "Does that mean you're going to tell me about what happened to your brother?"

Jones's mouth dried up, leaving nothing but a bad taste on the back of his tongue. Reliving that pain, remembering the way Kincaide had been before he'd died surged hot as acid in his gut.

"You said if this was going to work, we had to be honest with each other," she said. "If that's not something you're willing to do, it's better I know now. Before either of us gets in too deep."

"His name was Kincaide. He was my foster brother." Though Jones wasn't entirely sure if that'd actually been his brother's birth name or one he'd picked up along the way. "We were both in the system for a few years before we ended up in the same house. I was nine. Him, twelve. We hated each other at first. Looking back, I think we were both just trying to come to terms with how we ended up there and took it out on each other any chance we got."

Maggie seemed to soften, losing some of the bite she used against getting close to anyone she didn't have to. Either because of what she'd gone through or a characteristic she'd spent years building up, he didn't know.

"I'm sorry. I've known kids in the foster system. I can't imagine how hard that must've been."

"I didn't know anything different by the time I met Kincaide. My parents ditched me at a fire station when I was two. I don't remember them. I spent a good chunk of my life wasting time trying to figure out why they decided they couldn't take care of me, but I've since come to realize sometimes family isn't where you come from. It's who you trust."

Jones felt the assault coming. The grief he buried by throwing himself into the field day after day.

"The first few weeks, Kincaide and I did nothing but throw punches at each other. We were insecure, didn't know where we would end up next. Didn't know if the social workers would have us pack our garbage bags in a day, a week, a month. We were two angry kids who were caught in survival mode every hour of every day, and after a while, the only thing we could count on were those fights we picked with each other."

Maggie pressed her back into the wall, lowering herself onto the cold tile floor, and Jones wanted nothing but to scoop her up and put her back in that hospital bed. Only, he knew she wouldn't go. That she wouldn't admit defeat. "But you came to care about each other?"

He could see the moment his and Kincaide's relationship changed as though it'd happened mere minutes ago. "We were headed home after school. Our foster mom insisted we walk together, especially since I was younger, but I thought I was better than that. I'd always try to beat him home, then rub it in his face. I remember I'd gotten a new watch for my birthday. You know, the kind with the calculator built in. I was bragging to anyone who would listen all day about it because it was the best gift I'd ever received."

He still had that watch, tucked safely back in his room. "Well, these kids—I don't even remember their faces—jumped me a block from the house. They'd been waiting for me to pass by this dumpster to take it. I'd learned how to hold my own over the years, but it was three against one. I ended up curled in a ball while they beat the crap out of me."

Maggie's gaze glistened a split second before she swiped at her face with busted knuckles. "You must've been scared."

"I was. It was the first time in my life I remember thinking, I'm going to die. All for a stupid watch." Jones could almost feel every kick to his ribs, every fist that landed against his face. But there was something else. "Until my big brother came."

"Kincaide?" she asked.

"He wiped the floor with them. Got my watch back, though it'd been destroyed in the scuffle." Jones scratched at Gotham's neck with one thumb. "But I didn't care. Because I got something worth a lot more that day. I got a brother. Kincaide was pulled from that house because of that fight, but we didn't care. One of the kids' parents pressed charges, but it didn't matter where we were shipped off to. Nothing was going to stop us from having each other's backs. We wrote letters and called each other on our birthdays. Even after he went into the military, he made sure I knew I could count on him. I followed him, of course. Straight to the army as soon as I turned eighteen. Every few months I'd get word of where he was, but a couple years ago, the messages stopped. And I knew something had happened."

Maggie's expression fell. "In my room, you said you knew what I was going through. Is that because..."

"It took some digging. Me calling in every favor I

could over the course of two months, but I finally found my brother's last location." Jones tried ignoring the sick feeling in his gut, but there wasn't enough Pepto-Bismol in the world to touch that nausea. "Turned out Kincaide had been taken captive by a group of insurgents after an operation gone wrong. And the military couldn't do anything about it without starting a war." He notched his chin parallel to the floor. "So I did."

Chapter Five

He was going to be her source.

Maggie shuffled into a galley-style kitchen that'd been upgraded with chef-level appliances, beautiful countertops, sleek cabinets and expensive tile. It seemed everything about this place followed the same theme: the best of the best. Including the men and women operating out of this building.

"Our logistics coordinator takes her job very seriously." Jones ducked into the refrigerator ahead of her, pulling a stack of what looked like prepackaged food from one of the shelves. In her limited vision around his muscular frame, she caught at least four rows deep of those containers. "She tries to make sure we're not living off protein bars and shakes by putting together meals throughout the week. You want a Mediterranean bowl or peppercorn beef tenderloin?"

Her mouth watered at the possibility of having both. Right before her stomach knotted with hunger. Her body was working overtime, trying to repair the damage sustained over the past week. That took extra calories, but she wasn't exactly sure what her role here as guest entailed. Taking more than her share broke social conventions. At the same time, she could've probably eaten that entire refrigerator full of food. "I didn't think deciding what to eat would be such a tough choice."

"Then you can have both." Jones set the dinners—though was it dinner at four in the afternoon?—on the countertop and hunted for another meal. "I'll heat these up and bring them to the table."

"I can help." Her left leg thought otherwise, but she wasn't going to let Sosimo Toledano get the best of her. Not after she'd come this far. Maggie pried the lid of the Mediterranean bowl free, instantly craving the seasoned couscous beneath the fragrant chicken and tomato mixture. She made quick work of shoving the package into the microwave and hitting start as Jones withdrew from the refrigerator with his own serving in hand. She wasn't really sure what to do, what to say, as the countdown ticked off on the digital screen. She dug her fingernails into her palms—right where the pierced skin had started healing—and forced herself to release before she hurt herself all over again. "I'm sorry about your brother. About what happened to him. You said the military couldn't do anything to recover him without starting a war."

"Kincaide had been caught over enemy lines." Jones set his lower back against the counter, taking up so much space in the undersized kitchen, she felt small in comparison. Though not intimidated. Thick muscle banded beneath his T-shirt as he crossed his arms over his chest. He stood there, every ounce the operative she'd read up on when coming on board for *American Military News*.

"From what I'd been able to put together, he and his unit were assigned to pull a confidential informant out. It was all under the table. No official reports. Nothing on paper. The US wasn't supposed to be there, but this source was too valuable to let him get caught by his own people."

Maggie rested her weight against the opposite counter, facing him head on. His boots nearly touched her socked feet in the limited distance between them. And wasn't that the perfect comparison between them? He was solid, reliable, the kind of man who stayed on the defense while she'd rather curl up in bed and hide until the hard things went away. "But his unit was ambushed?"

"It was a setup. The informant turned on Kincaide and the others. Led them straight to their capture. In most cases, their deaths." Jones seemed to lose himself for a series of breaths. "Sending a unit to retrieve them would've been seen as an act of war. The US wasn't supposed to be there in the first place. Couldn't just ask for our hostages back without admitting we'd crossed the line."

The microwave shrieked, letting her know her first meal was hot and ready, but despite the invasive hunger carving through her, Maggie didn't move. "So you went after him?"

"Took some time." Two divots deepened between his eyebrows. Jones shifted his weight from one leg to the other. She could practically see his agitation at reliving those terrorizing memories, and Maggie wanted nothing but to close the distance between them. To offer some kind of comfort as he'd offered her the past four days. "I couldn't just up and leave my assignment when I heard. Nobody would tell me where he was. I had to call in a few favors to get the intel, and even then, I didn't have any support. No team. Superiors telling me it was all out of my purview."

"How did you manage to get him out of there?" The answer was already there, at the front of her mind. In the way he'd fought to get her out of *Sangre por Sangre*'s grasp. How he'd risked his life and Socorro's reputation protecting her. Jones Driscoll wasn't just doing a job. He was the kind of man willing to go down with the ship to save a relationship. The kind of man who put off his own needs in the face of his team's well-being. Who would disregard direct orders for the chance to save a life and didn't want anyone else making decisions for him and the people he cared about. The kind of man she only believed existed in fairy tales.

"I had a contact in the country. He got me over the border with an alias. Provided weapons, a satellite phone and an extraction." Jones seemed to come back to himself then, hiking himself away from the counter as he collected her heated food from the microwave. He somehow managed to make his movements look graceful despite his size. Something she'd never been good at, even though she was a hundred pounds lighter. "Took two days of surveillance to determine the hostiles were keeping Kincaide and another soldier from his unit in these underground tunnels. I had to go in hard. Take out as many combatants as I could in the first two minutes, but when I got to the end… I didn't even recognize him."

The bruising and cuts around Maggie's face seemed to come alive then, reminding her that thirty-six hours ago, she hadn't been recognizable either. The swelling had contorted her face into something alien. "But you got him home. You saved your brother. Him and his teammate, right?"

"I got them home, but I didn't realize until later I'd only saved a part of him." Jones pulled a drawer free and handed off a fork along with her meal.

She nearly dissolved into the warmth coming from the container. It was little things like this she'd missed the most while being Toledano's captive. Warmth. Light. Someone else to talk to rather than be talked at. "What do you mean?"

"The man I pulled out of there looked like my brother, talked like him even, but that was where the recognition ended." He didn't bother heating up his own meal, just stabbed a fork into the center, and her heart threatened to squeeze her to death. "He'd suffered several brain injuries in the weeks he'd been captive, to the point he'd forgotten big stretches of his life. He couldn't remember certain words. Sometimes he'd start talking, then lose track of what he was saying."

Maggie didn't have the stomach for couscous anymore. Her mouth dried up with the realization of why Jones had gone to such lengths to pull her out of *Sangre por Sangre*'s headquarters the way he did. Why he'd put so much time and energy into ensuring she recovered from her injuries. Why he paid attention to every word out of her mouth. "He didn't know you anymore?"

"No. He didn't." A reservoir of despair flooded into his expression. "Within a few months, the scar tissue building in his brain got so bad he lost fine motor control. He had to be put on a ventilator and a feeding tube. And I knew he didn't want to spend the rest of his life like that. I knew if he'd had the choice, he would've wanted to die in that ambush with his team rather than live the rest of his life in a hospital bed. He wouldn't have wanted me to sit by him hoping he'd snap out of it. So I did what I had to do."

She set her meal aside on the counter and, no longer able to keep her distance, reached out. Hesitant, careful. Her fingers skimmed along his arm, giving him the chance to pull away if he needed. Only he didn't. He didn't move, didn't even seem to breathe at her touch. She threaded her hand between his arm and rib cage, securing him in a hug. "I'm so sorry, Jones."

His hand found her shoulder blade, and within seconds the past few days diminished to a distant memory. Something she'd witnessed but hadn't lived through. Because of him. His resiliency, his concern, his drive to support the people in his life. And she needed that. More than she wanted to admit.

"How's the leg?" he asked.

"Stronger, I think." The lie left her mouth easier than she expected. In truth, her toes had gone numb since leaving her hospital bed, but she didn't want to give him another reason not to see this through. Without her to interrogate, Toledano would have started look-

ing for that SD card, if he hadn't already. There were
only so many places she could've hidden it in the short
seconds between him and his men killing those soldiers
and her racing to escape. He'd find it, sooner or later.

Unless she and Jones got to it first.

Jones unwound his arm from around her, and Maggie instantly missed the steady beat of his heart in her
ear. Which was ridiculous. She wasn't in a position or in
the right mindset to want anything more than a source
at this point in her life. She'd spent years disconnecting
herself from everyone around her. Her ex, her parents,
her siblings—anyone who'd abandoned her in the divorce. She didn't need or want attachments that would
get in the way of this new life she'd built for herself.
But she couldn't ignore that deep loneliness either. Or
that Jones seemed to ease that ache.

"You should eat up." Jones nodded toward her discarded food on the countertop. "We've got a lot of work
ahead of us."

"Right." She grabbed the container and forked a
heaping pile of couscous into her mouth. But Maggie
had a feeling eating enough wasn't going to be the biggest hurdle they went up against.

Jones scanned through the satellite images for the
tenth—or was it the eleventh?—time. Six nights ago.
That was when Maggie had said she'd followed the
cartel into the desert, that Sosimo Toledano had ambushed and murdered ten American soldiers to prevent
his own capture.

Only that wasn't what the satellite had recorded.

As far as he could tell, there was nothing out there. How the hell was that possible? Or was there something Maggie wasn't telling him? Maybe she'd gotten the days mixed up. It was impossible to keep track of time in survival mode, when every second of every day threatened to pulverize you. But going back another couple days didn't produce anything either. Jones double-checked the dates as low voices registered from the news report on the TV across the room.

Maggie had turned it on and promptly fallen asleep on his bed after they'd finished dinner. Gotham curled up next to her, despite knowing the bed was off-limits to fur balls like him, and Jones couldn't help but feed into the jealousy as he watched the two of them asleep now. Seemed he wasn't the only one breaking the rules.

Jones took in the latest news report. No one was reporting on this. No one had noticed a war correspondent had even gone missing. Or knew that Maggie Caddel was alive. This didn't make sense. Someone would've noticed. While he knew the full effect of the military's need for confidentiality, Maggie's abduction would've at least made local news. So why hadn't it? Surely her boss would have reported it. Someone who knew her.

He unpocketed his phone from his cargo pants and scrolled through the contacts. Hitting the name and number for Alpine Valley's chief of police, he darted for the door and closed it softly behind him, watching to ensure Maggie didn't wake up in the process. The line rang once then connected. He kept his voice low. "Halsey, it's Jones. I need a favor."

"And here I thought you were checking in on me." Baker Halsey had become one of the only outsiders Jones trusted to get to the truth. Halsey headed the massive cleanup of the landslide that had buried a quarter of Alpine Valley after a bombing meant to kill him and Socorro's logistics coordinator. He would do anything to protect his town. Something Jones wanted him to do now. "What do you need?"

"Maggie Caddel. You know the name?" Jones checked to make sure the door was still secure behind him. He moved farther down the hall. As much as he believed every word out of Maggie's mouth, trauma altered so many facets of truth and perception. He had to cover all his bases.

"Sounds familiar. I think she left me a message once. You know, before my phone and the whole police station got blown to hell a few weeks ago," Halsey said. "She's a reporter or something like that, right?"

"Yeah. *American Military News*. Has there been a missing person report filed on her? Anyone coming to the police asking about her or her whereabouts?" Because a woman didn't just up and disappear without anyone noticing. She had family, friends, coworkers, neighbors. Someone had to know something was wrong when she didn't come home.

"Not that I know of, but I'm not really handling the day-to-day while we try to clean up this mess. That mostly goes to my deputies." There was a deafening silence before Halsey's next question. "Why? Is this Caddel lady in some kind of trouble?"

"Something like that." Jones was missing something.

He could feel it. "Listen. Can you get in touch with your guys? See if her name comes up? Check with Albuquerque PD, too. Nothing official. Try to keep it off the books."

"Sure." Halsey's voice lost the lightness the chief had taken on since partnering up with Jones's teammate, Jocelyn. "But do you want to tell me what's going on first?"

"I'm not sure yet." The muscles in his spine tightened disk by disk as his bedroom door cracked open, putting Maggie in his sights. Jones held up his index finger to buy him another minute. "Find out what you can."

He ended the call before Halsey could ask too many questions Jones didn't know how to answer. He trusted the chief to come through. The ambush Maggie described couldn't just be swept under the rug. Not without leaving some kind of evidence behind.

Maggie left the safety of his bedroom, her foot still slightly dragging behind her right. "Everything okay? I woke up and you were gone."

"Yeah. Everything's fine." He tucked his phone back into his pocket. "Just checking in with the local chief of police. How are you feeling?"

"Better. Thanks. It's amazing what a nap and a shower can do for the soul." She set the side of her head against the wall as she leaned into it for support. How the woman was still standing after everything she'd been through, Jones didn't know. He couldn't even imagine how much strength it took.

"I thought that was chicken soup," he said.

"I'll take that if you have it, too. Even after both of those meals you gave me, I still feel like I could eat." Her smile tugged at one side of her mouth and washed the heaviness from her expression in an instant, but Jones had the distinct impression it didn't come as easy as it looked. As though she'd reserved it just for him. "Did the police have anything to say about what happened?"

"No. Nothing yet." His phone vibrated from his pocket, but his smartwatch said he'd regret answering. Ivy Bardot wanted answers, and as one of her operatives, he was required to give them. And he couldn't hold her off anymore. "My boss is calling. I'll need to meet with her, give her a rundown of what's going on."

"I understand. Go. Gotham and I will be fine. Just bring me back something to eat if you can. I'm starving." Before he had a chance to comprehend his next move, Maggie reached out, brushing her hand along his forearm. "Good luck."

The feel of her skin against his triggered a subatomic reaction in his nervous system, putting him instantly at ease. History and training had convinced him he could only feel that kind of effect in the middle of the battlefield or an operation, but this was different. More intense. Warm, even. "Thanks."

Jones watched as she retreated into his bedroom and closed the door behind her before he navigated two floors up to Socorro's founder's office. He knocked on the solid wood door but didn't wait for an answer, shoving inside. "You rang."

Ivy Bardot shuffled through the stack of paperwork

in her hands. Low eyebrows matching fiery red hair refused to budge as she took in whatever information she was reviewing. "You've been busy over the past couple of days from what I can see. Made a friend, too. Tell me about her."

Always to the point. Though, while Jones had been careful about how much information to give Alpine Valley's chief of police, Ivy Bardot most likely already knew everything he was about to brief her on. Lying, even by omission, was pointless, but more than that, Jones had no reason to keep information from her. The former FBI investigator had been hailed as one of the best, racking up more closed cases than any other agent in history before she'd peeled off from the federal government and founded Socorro, a defense against the country's most vile and violent organizations. One he was happy to be part of. Trusted. "Maggie Caddel, war correspondent for *American Military News*. I found her half-dead at the cartel's hands three nights ago. I was going to come to you with this eventually. Just trying to sort out the details."

Ivy flipped one of the pages in her hand toward him. "You accessed the satellite footage of a stretch of desert from around the time you recovered her."

There was the investigator he'd always admired. The one who'd proven time and time again how to put the puzzle together long before anyone else. Jones dared a step forward, needing movement, something to distract his brain from the unease circling through him. "Maggie claims to have witnessed the slaughter of ten American soldiers the night she was abducted. She took photos. Hid the SD card out there in the desert right before the cartel found her."

"Claims." One word. That was all it took for Jones to reconsider everything he thought he knew about this investigation. Socorro's founder didn't believe in coincidence. She didn't trust investigations lacking evidence. And she didn't support assignments running off pure emotion. "These images you requested from our friends at the Pentagon don't show any activity in the area. Cartel or otherwise. That kind of operation would be hard to miss, especially with the loss of American lives."

"But not impossible." His theory didn't feel right, though. Like he'd missed something. That was the problem with satellite imagery—there were thousands of pixels invisible to the human eye. He needed more information. Something concrete. "She could be misremembering the time frame in which she was held. Or there's something more going on here. Something that might even be above our pay grade."

"Take a seat, Jones." Ivy leaned back in her expensive leather chair, not a single wrinkle daring to crease her navy pantsuit. "I understand why you pulled her out of there, got her medical attention. She needed help, and you provided it. I commend that in my operatives. I encourage it. Why else are we here if not to protect the innocent against *Sangre por Sangre*? I can even understand why you would want to see this through, despite the evidence contrary to her statement, but she is not your brother, Jones. If you take on this investigation, I need to know your regret isn't leading the way. That you will look at the facts."

Jones locked his grip around the ends of the chair arms. He forced himself not to let his ego respond. Because, yes, some part of him wished that he'd been able to save Kincaide, but the other... The other part suspected there was a lot more going on here than some journalist caught at the wrong place at the wrong time. "The cartel didn't detain, question and torture her for days on end for no reason, Ivy. They wanted something from her, and she didn't give it to them. You and I both know we can't just send her back out there without protection. They'll find her, and they'll finish the job. Maggie has been following *Sangre por Sangre* soldiers for a year. I believe her when she says there was an ambush that resulted in the murder of American troops, that *Sangre por Sangre* is trying to cover it up and that she has proof. I trust her."

"Then I suggest you and Ms. Caddel take a field trip back to the location she was abducted and find that proof." She motioned toward the door, and Jones shoved himself to his feet. Dismissed. Ivy called from behind. "But if you come back with nothing, I trust that you'll let this go. Before it's too late."

Chapter Six

The uneven landscape jarred her and the SUV to one side. The movement aggravated the ache along her spine. Maggie grabbed for the side door handle, but no amount of force was going to keep her from being thrown around like Gotham's favorite chew toy. Stars punctured the black velvet sky through the windshield. If they weren't headed to the same location where she'd been abducted, she might've even thought it was beautiful out here. Peaceful. The perfect place to escape the noise and violence and pressure of the world. And in her head.

Her throat constricted as she stared out into the endless black. There were no towns out here. No sign of Socorro's headquarters. Nowhere they could run if this went sideways. Before the cartel had dragged her kicking and screaming into an SUV just like this one, that wouldn't have bothered her. She'd relished being on location, lived for the excitement of breaking a new story that might catapult her further away from her old life. Even prided herself on the danger of that kind of solitude. But now... Now she was grateful she didn't have to come out here alone. That she didn't have to do this alone. It was an odd shift compared to the past two years.

Maggie studied Jones in her peripheral vision. It was hard not to. He took up so much space, armored in Kevlar and banded muscle. The prickling sensation in her foot had spread, burning up her left calf. She'd been instructed to inform Dr. Piel of any changes, no matter how insignificant, but the promise of proving to Jones and every *American Military News* reader she wasn't crazy had hooked in deep. Besides, directing her thoughts on memorizing everything she could about the man next to her seemed to take the sting out. For now. "Thank you. For doing this. For believing me. Doesn't seem like your team agrees."

Jones stared out the windshield. No change in expression. Nothing she could read to give her an idea of what was going on behind that mask of his. He was evasive on a cellular level. Preferred to keep to himself, to work alone, but when it came right down it, he was the one who was here. Willing to fight beside her for the truth. "What makes you think that?"

"The fact that you're the only one from Socorro here with me." She tried not to cross her arms over her chest. Not only because it hurt like hell but to show that the realization didn't affect her. That she didn't actually need anyone but herself. That she was enough.

"Hey. Gotham's part of the team, too, you know," he said.

"Right." How could she forget the husky asleep in the back seat? "I take it the meeting with Ivy Bardot didn't go as you'd hoped."

"Satellite imagery doesn't show any activity in this region going back three weeks." Jones cut his gaze to hers, but the dim light coming from the SUV's dashboard wasn't strong enough to highlight the gray of his eyes. "I have clearance to follow up—"

"But if we don't find anything, you have to cut me loose." The implication of that statement hit harder than she expected. She couldn't go back to Albuquerque. Not as long as Toledano wanted those photos. And local police had already proved time and time again they didn't have the manpower to handle the cartel. *Sangre por Sangre* had infiltrated and corrupted departments over the years. There was no telling how far the infection had spread. And without evidence or jurisdiction, Albuquerque PD had no reason to investigate what'd happened or to protect her. Maggie pressed her back into the seat to gain some kind of control, but she couldn't seem to even level her own breathing. "That's…not possible. You tracked the last location of my phone. I was out there. I saw what Sosimo Toledano and his men did to those soldiers. I didn't make this up."

"I know." Two words and a whole hell of a lot of confidence. "Ivy is using her contacts to try to get a read on any operations the military might've been running out here, but so far, she's been stonewalled. Which makes me think there's more to it than we thought. Is there anyone you could stay with until the heat dies down? A friend, family member? A neighbor even?"

"No." She shook her head as though that would do any good to fight the ice seeping into her veins. The pride she'd held on to—that barrier she'd created between herself and everyone she'd loved—didn't seem as strong anymore. Not since the abduction. "I don't have anyone."

"Everyone has someone," Jones said. "What about your editor, maybe one of the other journalists?"

The suggestion almost made her laugh if it wasn't so sad. "I'm not sure if you understand how cutthroat my line of work is. We're all waiting for someone's life to fall apart so we can swoop in and claim what we think we're owed. To get ahead. We live for the scandals and discrimination lawsuits and sexual harassment charges. And my editor is at the top, fending off anyone gunning for his job. It's the only way to survive in this line of work. I wouldn't trust any of them with details of my life. Not unless I want to give them the upper hand."

"That doesn't sound like any way to live." Jones leaned back in his seat. Not relaxed or disengaged from the conversation. No. Something along the lines of pity.

She didn't need his pity. "You were in the military, and now you're an operator for a security company hired to deal with a drug cartel that kills dozens of people every day. You're constantly on the alert for a threat. I see the way you check the mirrors and how you've been sure to stay off the main roads. You're trying to protect yourself and Gotham. Isn't what I do the same thing?"

"Sure. When you look at it that way, but I still have my team. People who will have my back in an instant if I need them." His voice remained steady despite the earthquake shuddering through the vehicle as they crossed the desert. "What about your family? Do any of them even know you've been missing?"

"I'm not sure." She hadn't thought about her family in a while. Didn't even consider whether or not they'd be worried about her if the story of her disappearance broke, but nothing had been reported yet. No one knew she'd nearly died at the hands of the very cartel she'd been investigating. "After my divorce, my parents, my brother and sister, my friends—everyone cut ties with me. I'm pretty sure they've been brainwashed into thinking I'm dangerous."

"You were married." Jones's voice didn't sound so steady anymore.

"For nine years." Though it seemed like a whole other life now. "I don't really know what happened. The divorce has been finalized for two years, and I'm still trying to make sense of it."

"I take it he's the one who filed," he said. "You had no idea he wanted out?"

"No. We hadn't been having any problems that I was aware of. We were just…going about our lives. Meeting in the middle a couple times a week for dinner. Weekends were always busy with projects around the house, but we managed to spend a couple hours together watching TV at night or streaming a movie." It was those rare moments she'd missed the most. Having someone to talk to, to just be there to listen to her. "I guess a lot of times it felt like we were living our separate lives. Him with his work and me with mine. Then one day, I was getting ready to go into the office, and my husband—ex-husband—told me I needed to make a stop on the way over. At his attorney's office. He'd filed for divorce. Wanted me to pick up the papers and sign them. No questions asked."

Jones didn't have anything to say to that.

"I was blindsided. I didn't know what to do. I drove to my parents' house. I was a mess, but I didn't even have the guts to tell them what'd happened. I missed work. I was a no-call, no-show, and I didn't realize it until I checked my voice mails later that they fired me for it." Maggie set her head in her palm, her elbow leveraged against the window. Her body temperature spiked with a rush of anger, but she wouldn't let it take control. She was better than that now. "When I got home, my ex and I got in this huge fight because I didn't pick up the divorce papers. He tried to leave, and I went to stop him by jumping on his back."

The steering wheel protested under Jones's grip. "Did he hurt you?"

"Not in the way you think. About five days later, he called the police, claiming he believed his life was in danger. He had me arrested. I went to jail." She traced a long laceration across the back of her hand. Some injuries were so clear. Others kept festering without her notice. "After that, I got to see what kind of man he really was. He drained our bank accounts, called everyone in my contacts list and told them what'd happened, that I needed help, that he didn't feel safe with me. He turned them against me. Convinced them I would hurt them, too."

The vehicle slowed to a stop, and Jones shoved the SUV into Park. Headlights cut through a group of scrub brush and cacti ahead, but Maggie suddenly didn't have the inclination to leave this protective bubble they'd created over the past few minutes. "Want me to hunt him down and break something important?"

She couldn't stop the smile tugging at the corners of her mouth. That was exactly what she wanted. "As much as I want to see that, I think the only way to destroy a man like that is to show him I'm better off without him. Though I have to say, getting kidnapped and interrogated wasn't exactly what I had in mind."

"Then let's get you that story. Show the bastard what he gave up." Jones shouldered free from the vehicle and rounded the hood. Waiting for her. And in that instant, she had the distinct impression he'd never give up something so valuable as a partner. That he would do whatever it took to keep his relationships going.

Maggie tried to take a deep breath, but the idea of being that partner—of being the one he focused all that intensity on—slid through her without permission. She forced herself out of the SUV. The area looked familiar despite the bland landscape, and a chill threatened to hold her back.

"This is the last location your phone pinged," he said.

She moved as though a gravitational pull was tugging her closer. Then froze. Here. Lowering to her knees, she fanned one hand over the dry earth as Jones handed her a flashlight. Claw marks in the dirt. She could still feel the tension in her hands as she tried to fight back. She drove the beam down into a medium-sized crack, desperate to bury the memories. This was it. This was where she'd hidden the SD card. Maggie wedged her fingers into the small cavern. Only…she came up empty. Panic infused the muscles down her spine as she searched again. "There's nothing here."

CHUNKS OF CRACKED earth dissolved under his weight as Jones knelt beside her with another flashlight. "Let me take a look."

"I don't understand. It was here. I'm sure of it." Maggie didn't wait for his assessment and shoved herself to her feet. Spinning in circles, she lunged for another divide in the dirt and dropped to her knees. Dust rained down behind her as she practically clawed the ground to find the SD card. "It was here."

The desperation in her voice cut through him, and in that moment, Jones wanted nothing more than to produce the small device she'd claimed she'd hidden from *Sangre por Sangre* that night. He cast his flashlight across the ground, picking up two lines of drag marks. His gut clenched as his mind automatically imagined Maggie as the source. Footprints too. Not left behind by boots as he expected. More like dress shoes. But something else caught in the beam, reflecting back at him. Something that didn't belong out here.

"I didn't make it up." Maggie's voice turned distant. Uneven. "I didn't make it up."

Every cell in his body focused on the glassy surface caught at the base of a weed a few feet away. Jones knelt and reached through the spiny, dead branches to retrieve whatever it was. The broken edge bit into his thumb as he dragged it free. A circular piece of glass.

Not just any glass. Like the lens from a camera. Maggie's camera.

He pushed to his feet, offering her the shard. "No. You didn't."

Maggie stared at the clear lens before stretching a shaking hand to take it. As though simply touching it would ignite a frenzy of memories she didn't want to relive, and hell, Jones didn't blame her. "My camera broke on the rock when I fell, but the SD card isn't here. Toledano or one of his men must've already found it."

"If that's true, I'd be seeing a lot more activity around here." Jones scanned the ground for something—anything—that would tip off the cartel's presence. But whoever'd recovered that card had clearly gone to lengths to clean up after themselves. He wasn't seeing any treads left by vehicles or a flurry of movement on the ground. His beam caught the footprints he'd clocked a minute ago. It'd always been easy to spot the cartel's movements around any given scene. Poorly trained soldiers moved in packs, and *Sangre por Sangre* didn't bother with trying to cover up their crimes. They displayed them as a warning to anyone brave enough to take a stand. So who the hell would come out into the middle of the desert in dress shoes?

Jones headed back to the SUV and pulled a shovel from the cargo area, leaving the hatch open for Gotham. He couldn't go back to Socorro empty-handed. Not with Maggie's life still in danger. "You said you watched Sosimo Toledano and his men bury the bodies of the American soldiers. If that's true, Gotham will find them."

The husky shot ahead into the dark.

Jones fell into line behind her as she cut through a grouping of dried, spindly bushes. Even in the limited light from the SUV's headlights and their flashlights, he noted the tightness along her neck and shoulders. All she'd wanted was a new life, one that she'd built on her own. Away from the man who'd taken her trust and ground it into dust with a trumped-up call for her arrest. A burn Jones had only experienced after the news his brother had been captured and the knowledge he'd lost the support of his government raged through him. There had to be something more out here. Something that would convince Ivy and the rest of the team Maggie was worth more than a cover-up they couldn't prove. Because she deserved it. Because she needed it. And Jones wanted to be a part of that. He wanted to make sure she got everything that would help her move on. To be her support when nobody else wanted to come near her.

She slowed to a stop just before what looked like a ridgeline that angled down into a bowl of dirt and weeds. Swiping her hair behind her ear, she stared down into a collection of dried, dead bushes. "This is where I hid."

He maneuvered to get a better look at the scuff marks in the loose dirt. Without rain, there were impressions. Perhaps where she'd planted her elbows for stability. A few branches of bush had broken clean off. Jones gauged the distance between here and the location where he'd recovered the broken lens. Nearly fifty yards. She'd never had a chance once the cartel had spotted her. "And the bodies?"

"There." She pointed down into the bottom of the undersized dust bowl.

A tinkling of Gotham's collar reached his ears. Jones took that first step, his ankle engaging to keep him from tumbling straight to the bottom. If they were going to find answers as to what happened the night of her abduction, he'd have to dig. But the thought of forcing Maggie to confront the faces of the men and women massacred right in front of her pulled him up short. "You don't have to do this. You can go back to the SUV."

Her gaze locked on a point past his arm. She notched her chin higher and washed the emotion from her face, every ounce the driven, competitive war correspondent he imagined she'd had to become. Only that wasn't all she was. He'd witnessed moments where that mask had cracked and let the woman beneath bleed through. Where she didn't put her feelings in a box and pretended they hadn't existed at all. Where she'd let him see the warmth that might've thrived before her world had come apart. Mere slices of time but ones that had stayed with him since he recovered her. "I'm a journalist. This is part of the job."

Right. Jones offered her his free hand to help her down the incline. They moved as one toward the bottom, and the pressure behind his sternum intensified with every step. His gut knotted in warning as he scanned the rim of the bowl. It was impossible to see any kind of oncoming threat from down here, but his instincts said the proof they needed wouldn't wait for them to come back in daylight. Unrooted weeds—

dug up and discarded every few feet—caught on his bootlaces. Someone had been out here. The floor of the bowl was churned with loose dirt. Jones kept to the perimeter and swept the flashlight over the dried-up soil. A pair of bright eyes shined back in the beam. Gotham barked loudly enough to alert anyone within a mile radius. Jones handed off his flashlight. "He's got something."

Stabbing the tip of the shovel dead center, he was surprised by how easily the metal cut through the earth. Jones tossed shovelfuls of dirt over his shoulder as Maggie took up position in his peripheral vision. This was it. All they needed was a single body to start a government-wide investigation. Maggie would get her story, and Jones could get rid of the sick feeling in his stomach every time he thought of Kincaide. He could fix this.

Only the deeper he dug, the more that hollow feeling spread. The wood of the shovel was slick with sweat from his hands. His knuckles threatened to break through the thin skin as his grip tightened. Harder and harder with every discarded weight of dirt.

Visibly agitated, Maggie fisted her hands at her side. "Anything?"

"Not yet." His lungs worked overtime to keep in rhythm with his attempts. Jones sidestepped the four-foot hole he'd dug and launched the tip of the shovel back into the ground in another location. Two times. Then a third. Lactic acid burned in his arms and down his sides as he struggled to catch his breath. "I'm not finding any bodies, Maggie."

K-9 Shield

"No… They have to be here." Her voice cracked on the last word as she tore the shovel from his grip. Maggie pressed her heel into the lip of the metal and kicked down, but her left leg wasn't strong enough to support her. She lost her balance and tipped sideways.

Jones launched to catch her before she fell, securing her against his chest. "They're not here."

"Yes, they are. Gotham said they are. We just have to dig deeper." She fought against his hold as he tried to pry the shovel from her grip, and he let her go. Stepping back, Maggie clung onto the shovel as though her life depended on it. And right then, it did. "They have to be here. Because if they aren't, then I have nothing. I'll be nothing, and I can't go back to being nothing, Jones."

She swiped at the tears escaping down her cheeks and speared the shovel back into the ground. Once. Twice. Each time, he read pain in her arms, in her legs, in her back. But she didn't stop. Not even when she'd dug her own spread of holes and came up empty. In her mind, she had to do this. To prove she could. To earn that feeling of control over her own life.

Blisters stung in an arc on his palms, but they wouldn't stop him from giving Maggie everything he couldn't give Kincaide. Jones closed the distance between them and set his hand on the end of the shovel. She tried to wrench away, but this time, he wouldn't let her. "I'll dig through the night if you need me to, Maggie."

The hardness in her expression collapsed the longer they stood there. Time didn't mean a damn thing right then, but this did. This connection they shared. This partnership.

"Thank you." She released her hold on the shovel and stepped back. Surrendering her personal mission to him. And he would take it. For as long as she needed. No matter how heavy it was. Because he could. Because she needed something to believe in again.

Jones ignored the flare of discomfort in his arms and hands as he worked in a grid pattern through every inch of dirt within the bowl. Minutes distorted into an hour. Into two. There was nothing out here. Gotham wouldn't have signaled unless he'd recovered a human scent, but whoever'd retrieved the SD card must've taken the bodies. And with them, everything Maggie needed to get her life back.

"Stop, Jones." Maggie stared at the mess they'd made from the edge of the dig site. Her strength had failed her sometime during the past few minutes, leaving her paler than before. "You were right. There's nothing out here. No matter how much I want there to be."

His heart threatened to beat straight out of his chest as he let the shovel fall to the earth. Truth was, he didn't know how to do this. Be a partner. Wasn't sure what he was supposed to say or do in moments of despair, but he'd try. For her. "Maggie, I—"

A red light registered from the rim of the bowl.

Jones launched himself between Maggie and the potential threat.

Just as a gunshot exploded through the night.

Chapter Seven

Maggie wasn't prepared for the crushing weight of Kevlar slamming into her.

Her lungs collapsed under the attack. Her heart rate rocketed into her throat. A crack of thunder distorted Jones's voice as he ripped her off the ground and shoved her up the incline. No. Not thunder. A gunshot. Someone had taken a shot at them. "They found me."

Jones was still yelling orders at her, but she couldn't hear through the high-pitched ringing in her ears. He seemed to use his body as a shield between her and the shooter as he pushed his hand into her lower back. Her leg threatened to collapse straight out from under her, but he somehow made up for the difference.

Maggie slapped her hand on flat ground as they reached the rim of the oversize crater and dug her fingernails in to get a good grip. Only she didn't have to drag herself over the lip. Jones was already pushing her upward.

"Run for the SUV, Maggie. Don't stop. Not even for me." His mouth was close to her ear, and a pool of dread liquefied at the base of her spine. His voice remained even as he unholstered his weapon and took aim at the invisible threat. "I'll cover you. Go!"

Two shots. Three. The gun kicked back in his hand, but the force didn't even seem to faze him. Not like the shotgun rocking against her shoulder the night of her escape. This was the soldier in action. Socorro's combat controller. The one she'd been too traumatized and injured to appreciate when he'd pulled her out of *Sangre por Sangre*'s hands. This was the man who'd risked treason and death to save his brother—and paid dearly for it.

"I'm not leaving you here!" Maggie scrambled to her feet. The SUV's headlights cut through the night, but they suddenly seemed much farther than she'd originally estimated. Pressure intensified in her ears as bits and pieces of the night she tried to run for her life took control. Fear snaked into her brain and spiked her senses. The numbness in her left leg pricked at the back of her knee and held her hostage. Dryness scratched along her throat. She couldn't move, couldn't breathe. In an instant, her body betrayed her.

"Maggie, you've got to go!" Jones latched onto the back of her scrub top and pushed her forward.

She wanted to. More than anything, but her body suddenly had lost the ability to obey her commands. Gravity sucked her feet against the earth, trying to drag her into the sandy depths. Holding her back. And she wanted to let it. She wanted to disappear and pretend that none of this was happening. That she could do something for the lives lost here that night. Her lungs hurt. She couldn't get enough air. No matter how many steps Jones forced her to take.

A red dot zipped ahead of her. Then steadied.

"Get down!" Strong hands dragged her off her feet. Jones tucked her into his side and rolled, and all she could do was hold on to him for dear life. They landed in a sticker bush that bit through her clothes and pulled at her hair, but it was nothing compared to the pain that would've come with a gunshot.

The stars overhead streaked into her vision as another bullet kicked up dirt after impact. Mere inches from her head. Her protector returned the assault, but even with her limited knowledge of weapons, she knew his ammunition was running out. What felt like minutes sped up into distorted seconds until she couldn't distinguish one moment to the next. It was all a jumble that threatened to shut her down for good. There was only one way out, as she'd taught herself in the days in Toledano's hands. One way to make the pain go away. Maggie tightened her fist around the shoulder of his vest, desperate for something real to hold on to as her mind went to that numb place and started to detach from her body. "I can't go back."

Putting himself between her and the gunman, Jones dragged her to face him. "I'm going to get you out of this, but I need you to do everything I say. Understand?"

Another red beam cut through the night and crept up the side of Jones's neck. The gunman had him in his sights. She'd done this. In an instant, she'd put them in a position to lose. And they were out of time.

"Stay with me, Maggie." His jolt shuddered through her, and the numbness she wanted so badly drained away. Jones's hold on her was too strong. Too real and impossible to ignore. "I need you to trust me."

Trust. She didn't trust anyone. Not even her own family and friends—people who'd known her all her life. Who'd let themselves be manipulated and gaslighted by a handsome liar who'd built her up to be some kind of unstable attention seeker. But Jones... Jones wasn't like that. No. This was the kind of man who defended others far more and with more determination than himself. Who would give up anything for his team. And her. Even his own life. He'd already proven that, hadn't he? Her fingers rushed with blood as she released her grip on his vest. "I trust you."

"Then take Gotham and run. Now," he said.

The crack of another bullet screamed through the night.

Gotham raced ahead of her.

Maggie launched forward as a patch of dirt exploded at her feet. Right where Jones should've been. She couldn't look back. Couldn't assure herself he hadn't gotten caught in the cross fire. She pumped her legs as hard as she could take, and a cramp knotted at the back of her thigh. She made out the SUV's frame through the headlights ahead. Maybe fifty feet. She was going to make it. Her left toes caught on a protruding rock, but she wouldn't let it trip her up. She had to keep going. No matter what. Because as much as she trusted Jones to protect her, he trusted her to follow through with his commands. To get help.

She'd spent so long trying to prove she was worth something—to someone, anyone—that she'd forgotten what that felt like. To be valued. Feeling flooded into her legs and reinforced the last of her strength as she closed in on the SUV. Her hand slammed onto the hood as she ripped the driver's side door wide open.

Gotham launched into the back seat. His short claws scratched against the glass as she secured the hatch. He tried to get free of the vehicle when he realized Jones hadn't followed, but there was no way she was going to send him back out there.

"He's going to be okay." She had to believe that. Maggie hit the push-to-start, locking her and the husky inside. The engine vibrated at her feet, and she didn't waste any time launching the SUV into Drive. Momentum hauled her into the back of the seat as she flipped the vehicle back the way they'd come. "We're going to get help. Okay? We're coming back for him."

A second set of headlights cut through the night and beamed through the passenger's side window. No. Too strong to be manufacturer headlights. They had to be spotlights. Blinded by the onslaught, Maggie raised one hand to shield her vision. She couldn't make out the vehicle, but her gut said if she took her foot off the accelerator, she'd end up right back in that dank hole Sosimo Toledano had put her in. Maneuvering away from the source, she floored the pedal.

Another set of lights brightened ahead.

She turned the wheel so fast to avoid the collision, Gotham slid across the back seat with a stressed yip. Maggie shook her head as though that would somehow free her of the fear clogging her throat. Just as a third vehicle lit up its spotlights. She slammed on the brakes, and the SUV slid a dozen feet across the water-starved ground.

Surrounded.

It was an ambush. Toledano and his men had been waiting for her to come back for the SD card. Just as Jones had warned. There were too many of them to outrun on her own. Damn it. The photos, the bodies, her eyewitness account—anything that would prove the atrocities *Sangre por Sangre* had committed—would be extinguished if she didn't find some way out of this. Tremors shook through her hands as she slid her palms against the steering wheel. She was out of options, her best one being facing off with a shooter at least a hundred yards behind them.

Silhouettes of men filtered out of the vehicles, with one taking the lead. Her heart kicked in her chest as she automatically filled in the dark hole where a face should've been with Toledano's features. Other things came into focus then, too. The outline of guns registered through the spotlights. This SUV's windows were bulletproof. She'd already tested their strength, but that'd been with one weapon. Not an entire army ready to tear apart anything that got in their way.

The head figure started walking toward her.

The same survival instinct that'd gotten her onto her feet after Jones and Gotham had rescued her from the cartel slid in to take control. That blind fear threatened to steal logic as Maggie twisted around in her seat. The curve of the man-made cemetery took shape out the back window. One second. Two. No movement. Nothing to suggest Jones was alive, that he'd taken out the gunman or that he was on his way to her right now.

She'd left him to fight this battle alone. Like the coward she'd become during the divorce. Never wanting to have to sacrifice anything more than she had to. Waiting for someone to come and intervene, for a hero to knock down the door and fix the problem. That hope had died when her mom had stopped returning her calls, when the invites for nights out with girlfriends got fewer and farther between and coworkers avoided interacting with her in the office. When she'd somehow survived another day of interrogation. Jones had been that for her. Her knight in shining Kevlar armor.

But no one was coming this time. Her breath eased out of her chest as Maggie rammed the gearshift into Reverse. She didn't know what would happen, but she couldn't let Jones fight this battle himself. Not when she was the reason it'd started in the first place. "Hang on to something, Gotham. I think it's about to get really bumpy."

She slammed her foot onto the pedal.

He was pinned down.

Jones assessed the amount of ammunition left in his weapon. Not enough. The boulder at his back worked as cover for now, but any move on his part and that sniper would finish him off. He studied the blacked-out terrain spreading out in front of him. Maggie had gotten to the SUV. He could just make out the headlights swinging around.

Then another set.

And a third.

His pulse thudded harder as he took in the vehicles closing in around her. Oh, hell.

A bullet ricocheted off the rock mere inches to his left. Dust flicked up into his eyes, and Jones automatically raised his arm to protect his face. The sniper had the advantage here. Hold Jones hostage while the rest of the cartel got what they'd come for. Maggie. What he wouldn't give to get his hands on a rifle of his own.

The SUV skidded to a halt. Surrounded.

He wouldn't make it in time. *Sangre por Sangre* was going to take her.

And there was nothing Jones could do about it.

A section of the boulder jutted into his spine, and he pressed into the shard deeper to keep him in the moment. To stop the onslaught of failure from creeping in. He wasn't overseas. He didn't have to do this alone. And Maggie was going to make it through this. No matter what it took.

Jones tried to gauge the sniper's location without putting his head in the cross hairs. A bullet ripped through the ledge of rock and broke a chunk away. He would lose his cover in a matter of minutes.

Except the SUV was coming right at him. Backward. And it wasn't slowing down. Confusion barely had the chance to take hold before Jones was forced to evacuate his hiding spot. The vehicle slammed into the boulder standing between him and a sniper's bullet. The cargo tailgate snapped free. "Get in!"

He didn't have time to question Maggie's tactics as two more heavy rounds cut through the SUV's side panel. The back driver's side tire deflated beneath the vehicle's weight. Jones shoved to his feet and launched himself into the cargo area. He managed to grab onto one of the back seats as Maggie floored the accelerator. Gotham centered his head between the seats to get a look at Jones in the back. Throwing back the removable floor, he catalogued the weapons every Socorro operator was required to carry and pulled his rifle free. "What the hell are you doing? I told you to get out of here."

The back window caught a single bullet. Aimed directly at Jones's head.

"I tried!" Maggie wrenched the wheel to the left to avoid a head-on collision with another vehicle coming at them too fast. The SUV fishtailed and grazed along the truck's fender. Two more sets of headlights were headed straight for them as the third kept on their tail. "I'm not sure if you know this, but I'm not a very good driver. They took away my license. I didn't have any other choice."

"You don't have a valid driver's license?" Jones loaded a round into his rifle.

The truck on their tail surged forward. Metal screeched against metal as the two vehicles locked in a spar for control, but the windows held.

"Is that what you really want to be focusing on right now?" Maggie jerked the wheel into the other vehicle, to keep them from flipping. The truck was trying to guide them straight into the two up ahead.

Gotham slid across the back seat with a yip, his oversize paws attempting to grab on to anything solid. He fell behind the driver's seat but popped his head up a moment later. Probably loving the ride.

"I'm just saying that information would've been good to know before I got in." Jones braced his shoulders against the back seats and kicked at the compromised back window. The sniper bullet fell free before the window dislodged in one piece. Air rushed into the SUV as he wedged the butt of the rifle against his shoulder and took aim. Then pulled the trigger.

The bullet found its mark, taking out the back tire of the truck. The tail end swerved to one side, then caught against something on the desert floor. Shouts cut through the grind of engines as the driver of the truck failed to keep all four wheels on the ground. The truck flipped, landing with a gut-wrenching crunch. Jones unpocketed another round and loaded it into the rifle. "Anything else you think I need to know while we're trying to stay alive?"

"I'm allergic to dairy. Is that helpful?" She whipped her head around, then grabbed for Gotham with one hand, guiding the husky into the front seat.

"Only if the cartel tries to torture you with cheese." He leveraged the barrel of the rifle against the window frame and set his eye against the scope. "Slam on the brakes on my signal and turn right as hard as you can. Let off the accelerator at the curve, then get us up to speed when we've straightened out. The wheel will want to follow, but I need you to keep us steady. Understand?"

Maggie held strong, and he couldn't do anything but admire her sense of humor in a situation like this.

She wasn't trained for evasive driving, let alone combat, but she was meeting him in the field regardless. Most civilians would've given up by now. But she was a fighter. "Did you miss the part where I said I'm not a good driver?"

"You're doing just fine. Remember what I asked. I need you to trust me. This will even the odds." Jones settled into that familiar space. The one created over years of missions and violence and death. He'd relied on it so many times to get him through whatever lay ahead. Only this time felt different. It felt more personal than ever before. The rocky landscape threatened to loosen his grip on the rifle, but he wasn't going to let Maggie get captured again. He wasn't going to be too late this time. He was going to get her out of this mess. "Now!"

She hit the brakes. Momentum tried to rip him free of his position as Maggie wrenched the steering wheel to the right, and the SUV swung around, putting one of the approaching vehicles dead in his sights. The engine vibrated through the entire frame as the SUV launched forward.

Jones found his mark.

And compressed the trigger.

The bullet embedded in the front fender of the truck but didn't have any overall effect. He backed away from the scope. Damn it. He'd hit the target. It should've put the engine out of commission. Unless… "That truck's armored."

"What?" The question left Maggie's mouth a split second before the impact.

Time seemed to speed up and slow down all at once.

Maggie's head rammed toward the steering wheel just as the airbag engulfed her. Glass and metal protested from the passenger side where Gotham had been sitting a moment before. The world barrel-rolled once. Twice. Three times. Gravity lost its hold on his body, and Jones was flung between the two back seats. Upholstery failed to cushion each blow as the SUV battled against the earth's physics. He tried reaching for the front seat, but blood clouded his vision. He couldn't see her. Couldn't touch her.

In an instant, Maggie was gone.

The ground rushed up to meet the driver's side of the SUV. The back seats pinned him in place, his feet grazing against the shattered side window and collection of artillery that'd come loose in the collision. Dust drove into his lungs as the vehicle came to a rest. Hell, his head hurt. He couldn't think, couldn't take a full breath. "Maggie, can you hear me?"

No answer.

The silence pressed in from every angle and shot his nerves into overdrive. He should've picked a bigger gun to get through the truck's armor. Now Maggie was in danger. Because of him. Because he hadn't been enough to protect her. Just as he hadn't been enough to get to Kincaide before it'd been too late. That echo of grief and loss cut through him. His eyes burned. He'd given Maggie his word he wouldn't let *Sangre por Sangre* get their hands on her again. How much was his word worth now?

"Gotham?" He couldn't hear the husky through the ringing in his ears. Jones reached toward the front center console, trying to claw free of the grip the back seats had on his middle. Pain radiated through his insides, but it wasn't enough to stop him from getting to his partner. Either of them. "You both better be alive."

A low rumble of an engine vibrated through what was left of the SUV's frame. Crushing realization hit him harder than the initial impact. The cartel was going to take Maggie. They were going to kill her. Because they no longer had reason to keep her alive. The SD card she'd buried had been recovered, the bodies they'd tried to hide removed from the site. He was going to lose her.

"Jones..." A section of blond hair fell from around the driver's seat headrest. A shaking, bloodied hand pawed at the airbag, and white powder kicked up in a fresh beam of headlights. She was alive. Against all the odds, she'd survived the accident, and something he didn't realize had been squeezing the life out of him released.

"I'm here, Maggie. I'm coming for you. Just hang on. Okay?" he said.

Voices registered from outside the vehicle. A burst of footfalls rocketed Jones's instincts higher. Three, maybe four sources. Moving fast and coming right for them. They had mere seconds. He latched onto the two front seats and hauled the rest of his body free of the back. Black-and-white fur demanded his attention from under the passenger airbag on the floorboards. Gotham. Jones brought his oversize frame into the front and scooped the dog into his chest. Gotham's pulse kicked against his palm. Alive.

Rock and glass peppered Maggie's scrubs, but the only blood seemed to be coming from a laceration down her arm. Jones swept her hair out of her face to get a better view with his free hand. "Stay with me. I'm going to get you out of here."

"It's too late." She lifted her injured arm and pointed out the windshield. Silhouettes paired off, growing bigger as they approached. "They're already coming."

The driver's side window exploded.

Chapter Eight

Her shoulders were pulled tight.

They protested as though they were about to disconnect from their sockets. She was moving. Though Maggie didn't understand how that was possible. The crash. The airbag. Gotham diving for the floorboards. Jones. Fractures of memory jumbled until she wasn't sure of the order, but they were all there.

Her bare heels dragged against the ground. She tried lifting her head to gauge where she was, but something scratchy and tight dulled her vision. Her exhales collected just in front of her mouth and nose. A bag. Toledano had used a bag. He'd enjoyed keeping her guessing as to where the next strike would come from.

Maggie dug her fingernails into her palms and pulled at her hands, trying to gain some semblance of control. "No. No, please. Don't take me back."

Whoever had a hold of her hands didn't slow, didn't stop. Didn't even seem to hear her. Or care. Her jaw and cheekbones ached with every word, but she wasn't going to go back into that hellhole without a fight. Not again. Rocks cut through the thin scrub top, scratching along her skin. She dropped her head back between her arms as a sob built in her chest. "I don't have what you want. I'm telling the truth. Please."

"Quiet." The voice grated against her nerves. Too rough. No accent. Not one of the soldiers who'd questioned and tortured her before. There were outsiders within the organization she'd learned about over the past year of investigating. Contractors hired to carry out a variety of jobs. Executions, frame jobs, undercover work within other cartels or within police departments. At least, according to the rumors. She hadn't been able to make heads or tails of any of it. Not without exposing herself. *Sangre por Sangre*'s management was careful. Neither local law enforcement nor the feds had any luck either. And now, she was going to be one of those cases that got lost in some file room. Just waiting for someone to come along and make the connection.

Fear pricked at the back of her neck as the man dragging her suddenly let go. Blistering heat singed her arm hairs, and Maggie tried to roll away from the soft glow through the fabric of the bag over her head. In vain. Strong hands wrenched her to her feet and pinned her against a wall of muscle twice her size. The bag was torn from her head, taking a few strands of hair with it. She winced against the brightness of the roaring fire.

"Maggie Caddel. I've been looking for you." Masculine features darkened from the onslaught of the flames as a man approached. The bonfire was on the verge of reaching at least fifteen feet in the air, but not one fueled by wood alone. No. A distinctive sour odor lodged at the back of her throat as she took in the masked faces of the men and women circling the fire. Six. All heavily armed. None of them Jones. "I've got to say, you've given me and my unit a lot of grief lately."

Unit? *Sangre por Sangre* didn't work in units.

"Am I supposed to take that as a compliment?" Her voice broke on the last word, giving away the terror and confusion clawing through her. She'd survived interrogations, starvation, dehydration and physical torture from a cartel lieutenant, not to mention a night in jail on a faulty assault charge, yet there was still a part of her that hated her weakness showing through under intimidation. Maggie jerked against the hands holding her in place, but it was no use. Every single one of these soldiers was so much…bigger than she was. Stronger. Faster. She didn't have a chance against any of them. A bone-deep ache resonated through her shoulders at the pressure. "The man who was with me. Where is he?"

"He ain't coming for you, sweetheart." A hint of a Southern drawl filtered into the man's voice as he crossed his arms over a vest similar to Jones's. Though, not the same in color. Other distinctive features bled into focus as he stepped into her personal space. The watch on his left wrist. It wasn't one of those complicated gadgets that read data and synced with other devices. Simply an analog with a brown leather strap that'd seen a thousand lifetimes. Inherited, if she had to guess. Important. "Turns out, your new friend is former military. Emphasis on the former. Something about disobeying direct orders and crossing into enemy territory. Lieutenant Driscoll almost started a war with his little stunt to pull those soldiers out of that cave. Me and my guys? We don't cross the line. We know that compromising an assignment gets people killed."

"Jones. His name is Jones." The haze fogging her brain after the accident was cracking. Maggie tried to step free of her captor, but that only made him dig his fingers deeper into her arms. "But you called him lieutenant. Like you think you're supposed to. You're… you're military. All of you."

Hope lit up behind her sternum at the thought of the army responding to the ambush that led to her abduction by a drug cartel. Then faded. "Wait. You said you and your unit don't disobey orders. What part of your orders were to shoot at and endanger two US citizens tonight?"

"You really don't know when to stop asking questions, do you, Maggie?" The dark ski mask failed to hide a thin five-o'clock shadow around the soldier's mouth. "You think uncovering the truth will make everything better, but I can tell you from experience, that's almost never the case."

The use of her name—so intimate, as though they were old friends—hit her nerves wrong. Nothing compared to when Jones said her name. Her stomach threatened to revolt. Her skull bounced against her captor's chest in rhythm to his heart rate. Which had just jumped a few beats. Pressure tightened in her gut at the change. Something was wrong. These men and women—military or not—weren't who she wanted them to be. "I don't understand."

"Then let me put it in terms you will understand." He got close enough she could smell a hint of deodorant as he threaded her hair out of her face. But not from under his arms. From his palms. To control any sweat that might leave his DNA behind. "That night you followed one of our units into the desert and took photos of an off-the-books operation, you became a liability. The people of this country rely on us being able to do our jobs, Maggie. That comes with a certain confidentiality we have to maintain. We can't have you risking their lives with your lies or recruiting others into your fantasy of what you think you saw that night. One life compared to thousands? It's not a hard choice."

The finality of that statement cut through her. Sharp and fast. Fantasy? No. She wrenched one arm free from the man at her back and lunged. Only to be brought back to heel. "Confidentiality. You mean cover-up, don't you? I didn't follow one of your units out there that night. I was investigating *Sangre por Sangre*. I know what I saw. I know the cartel ambushed and murdered ten American soldiers that night. I have proof. What I don't know is why you're okay with that. Why any of you are okay with that."

Jones had risked his life and his entire career for the soldiers who'd been captured behind enemy lines. But these men and women… They weren't the same. They weren't fighting for their country. They were fighting for themselves.

"Is this the proof you're talking about?" He unpocketed something from his cargo pants and held up an SD card. A perfect match in brand and size to the one she'd buried in the ground the night of her abduction. Then tossed it in the fire. "What proof?"

"No!" Maggie ripped free of her captor and went after the card. Heat painfully flared up her neck and burned across her face. It landed at the perimeter of the fire, its edges sizzling and smoking instantly. She collapsed to her knees—adding insult to injury in her left leg—and grabbed for a stick that hadn't caught fire. She tried to drag the card out, but within seconds, the blue plastic had melted in on itself, taking her future with it. Her throat burned. She turned on the leader. Struggling to her feet, she shoved his chest. Not even throwing him off balance. "Why would you do that? Those soldiers deserve justice. They deserve peace."

Anger she'd felt only once in her life exploded through her. Maggie shoved him again.

He caught her wrists in both hands. "Peace comes at a price, Maggie. A price me and my unit and every other enlisted soldier are willing to pay. Those men and women you claim you saw die that night? They knew that. They knew what they were getting into when they joined up, and they died heroes. You don't get to take that away from them or their families."

He returned her shove.

Maggie fell back. The impact jarred old injuries and aggravated new ones. The circle of soldiers seemed to close in, cutting off her escape. None of this made sense. "So what now?"

"I told you. We never break orders," he said.

Movement registered from behind the man standing over her. Flames highlighted two more men hauling something heavy between them. A body. Dressed in uniform. Maggie could do nothing but watch as they swung the load—back and forth—before releasing it into the flames. Sparks flew overhead and cooled against the black night sky. That smell, the one she'd noted a few minutes ago… It hadn't been accelerant as she'd believed.

It'd been human remains.

First, the SD card. Then the bodies *Sangre por Sangre* had buried in the pit that night. These soldiers—whoever the hell they were—were getting rid of evidence of the ambush. Only none of this made sense. Why would the US military clean up after a cartel slaughter? What good came of sacrificing ten American lives and letting an organization like this get away with it?

"It's done," a familiar voice said. Accented. Deep. It triggered a nuclear response in her nervous system and seized any thoughts of escape.

Her throat threatened to close in on itself as Maggie forced her attention to the newcomer maneuvering into the circle of light cast off by the bonfire. El Capitan wiped his hands on a stained bandanna as she'd watched him do so many times before, and her blood ran cold.

The masked soldier took a final step toward her and crouched, leveling that dark gaze with hers. "Good. Then that just leaves the last piece of the puzzle."

BROKEN GLASS CUT into the blisters in his palms as Jones pressed upright.

His head hit the dashboard and ignited the pain ripping through his skull. He wasn't supposed to be here. Maggie. He had to get to Maggie. The team that'd flipped the SUV had moved fast and gone straight for her. He hadn't even gotten the chance to fight back before one of them clocked him over the head from behind. Organized. Trained. Almost militaristic in strategy. *Sangre por Sangre* didn't move like that. Not in the dozen encounters Jones had survived. No. This... This was something else. Someone else.

Twisted metal and darkness stretched out in front of him. The windshield had somehow survived the accident, but the driver's side window was gone. Dry midnight air carried a hint of something unrecognizable into the cabin of the SUV. Hell. How long had he been unconscious?

A soft whimper drilled through the haze dimming his senses and spiked his blood pressure. "Gotham? Is that you, buddy?"

It came again, but he couldn't get eyes on the source with the passenger side airbag in the way. Pulling the blade from his ankle holster, Jones deflated the airbag in a rush of white powder and stale air. The dog's outline took shape along the floorboards. He tossed the blade onto the front seat and reached for his partner. Matted fur caught between his fingers as Jones carefully pulled Gotham into his arms. "It's okay. I've got you."

The husky tucked his dry nose into Jones's neck and licked the skin there. Jones checked him for injuries but found no blood or broken bones. The K9 had taken a beating though.

"Let's get you back to HQ." Compressing the emergency call button on Gotham's collar, Jones tucked his undersized sidekick beneath one arm. He reached for the driver's side door with his free hand, but his strength gave out. He dropped his shoulder first against the steering wheel. Pain ricocheted down his arm and into his chest. "That's going to leave a mark."

Time pressurized the air in his lungs. He wasn't sure how long ago the team that'd ambushed them had taken Maggie. Didn't know if she was injured. If she was alive. One thing was for certain: he wasn't going to leave her to fight this battle alone. He wasn't going to fail her as he'd failed Kincaide. His own life be damned.

Jones kicked at the driver's side door. Corrupted hinges protested as the door snapped back. He and the dog fell through the opening as one as he twisted to avoid landing on Gotham. The dog's paws braced against his chest as Jones surveyed what might be broken throughout his body. "I don't suppose you're carrying some ibuprofen."

Gotham cocked his head to one side.

"I'll take that as a no." He hauled the K9 off of him and forced himself to his knees. "All right. Help is on the way. You're going to stay here while I try to hunt down the bastards that took Maggie."

The husky's whine speared through Jones's resolve. Gotham didn't like being alone.

"I know." Jones stretched back inside the busted frame of the SUV and pulled his sidearm from the wreck. Dropping the magazine free, he counted the rounds left after dueling with a sniper back at the pit. Two. He was going to need more than that to take on a small army. "But you were damn lucky you didn't get hurt in the accident. I can't risk worrying about you while I'm trying to pull her out of...wherever she is."

Gotham didn't give an answer this time. Simply ducked his head and pressed his forehead to Jones's shin.

"You're not going to take no for an answer, are you?" Just as well. Leaving Gotham here ensured Socorro operatives would discover the K9 and the wreck through his emergency signal, but they wouldn't even know where to start to find Jones or Maggie by the time they arrived on the scene. "Fine. Come on."

The husky followed as instructed.

Jones rounded to the back of the SUV and collected all the ammunition and weaponry he could sustainably carry. He extracted his discarded flashlight and tested the power. Worked. Casting the beam over the desert floor, he picked up on four sets of footprints. One direction leading straight to the SUV. The other heading back where they'd originated. Boots. Heavy tread. He followed the line, realizing the number of prints didn't change, but the depth of one set got deeper. One of them had carried Maggie out. Which meant she'd either been bound or unconscious. Either way, she'd never had a chance to fight back. "Keep a nose out, dog."

The flashlight picked up two lines of ruts. Vehicle treads. Though there wasn't any sign they were within a mile of his location. The team that'd taken Maggie could be anywhere by now, but that wasn't going to stop him from getting to her.

Jones jogged to follow the treads, Gotham bouncing

in rhythm with every step. He wasn't sure how much time had passed or when his knee had started screaming for rest. Twenty minutes. Maybe thirty. But the warm glow up ahead told him he was headed in the right direction. The fire lit up a natural arch and unique rock formations, providing protection for the group camping at the base. The reddish color and eroded towering rocks took the formations straight out of some science fiction book set on Mars, but would allow Jones to approach from behind. As long as he kept his distance.

He slowed as a hint of something sour collected at the back of his throat. The odor threw him back to a mission set during his last official tour overseas. Where an entire village had been burned to the ground mere minutes before his unit arrived to help. That smell had stayed with him all this time. Not fueled by wood alone. But by human bones. "Maggie."

He couldn't see her from this distance. Jones circled the rock formations, cutting off his access to the group and hiking his nerves into overdrive. He didn't like not knowing what he was getting himself into, but his need to get Maggie out dominated his doubts. She was there. She had to be. Because if she wasn't… If she was already gone… No. He couldn't think about that. Jones hiked the incline leading to the arch—honed over hundreds of years—and slipped his hand through the middle to keep his leverage. Grains of coarse dirt dislodged in his hold, threatening his balance. But he gained a perfect view of the camp and the masked men and women circling the fire.

And of Maggie.

"Please, let me do the honors." Sosimo Toledano closed the distance between him and Maggie, setting all of Jones's defenses on high alert. He was outnumbered. Outgunned. Any move on his part could put her at risk, but doing nothing guaranteed it. "After all, Ms. Caddel and I are friends."

"Friends don't torture each other for photos." She shoved her hands into the ground to back away, but another of the gunmen ensured she couldn't escape. The man she knew as El Capitan reached for her arm. Maggie landed a solid kick to his shin, but it was no use. He latched onto her, hauling her into his chest. "No!"

Her scream bounced off the rock formations and etched deep into Jones's brain.

Jones unholstered his weapon and slid down the front of the arch on one hip to avoid colliding with Gotham. Then took aim. "Didn't your mama teach you no means no, Sosimo?"

Seven soldiers reached for their weapons. Jones only had attention for one.

He pulled the trigger. The bullet ripped through Sosimo Toledano's side and catapulted him away from Maggie. The man's screams cut through the night as the fire caught on the lieutenant's clothing. She covered her ears with both hands and ducked as Jones launched for her. He fisted one hand into her scrub top and swung her behind one of the smaller formations as cover.

The human torch formerly known as Sosimo Toledano ran straight for a handful of soldiers, but they had no compassion to help.

"You're making a mistake, Driscoll." One of the

masked soldiers took center stage, his unit at his back. Ah, this was the man in charge. Seemed Toledano had merely been serving a purpose, but with the cartel lieutenant running for his life, that left room for the real monster to show his face. American military, Jones guessed. At least, based off their formation and tactics. But did that make them former or current? He didn't know. "There's no way out. Maggie's gotten herself in too deep. There's no scenario that we let you walk away from here with her alive."

His heart pounded hard behind his ears as Jones calculated their chances. Okay. The guy behind the mask had a point, but if Jones had let himself accept defeat against the odds, his brother would've died in that cave and not with the people who'd loved him.

Taking a defensive stance, Gotham growled at the men putting Jones in their crosshairs with a flash of fangs.

A rolling laugh reverberated through the small circle of armed soldiers.

It was the distraction he needed.

Jones backed up, using his body as a shield for Maggie. "Then you haven't considered all of the scenarios."

One squeeze of the trigger. Then another. Each bullet found its mark, knocking two gunmen out of the lineup. The rest dove for cover and started to return fire. A round missed Jones's ear by mere millimeters as he took another step back. He whistled low to call Gotham then turned to Maggie. "One of their trucks is parked about a hundred yards west. Keys are in the ignition. We can make it if we run now."

Maggie's hand found his arm. A bolt of heat that had nothing to do with the growing bonfire burned through him, spurring adrenaline through his veins. "Just say when."

Jones took down another of the gunmen. "When."

They moved as one. Him as the shield, her navigating over the terrain. Four hostiles left their cover to follow, but he had one last trick up his sleeve to make sure that didn't happen. Jones pulled a flash grenade from his cargo pants. He detached the tab and tossed it straight into the bonfire. "Go, go, go!"

Maggie ran straight into the darkness with Gotham close on her heels.

The device exploded in a burst of light. The resulting blast wave knocked the last gunmen off their feet and sent bolts of fire in every direction. A guttural scream bounced off the rock formations, which threatened to tip at any second, but Jones wasn't going to wait to watch the aftermath.

"This isn't over, Driscoll!" The warning broke through the pop of flames. "We'll never stop coming for her. You can run, but you can't hide!"

Chapter Nine

A hiss ignited the sensitivity in her teeth as Socorro's physician added another stitch in Maggie's forearm. Could've been worse. She could've ended up burned at the stake with the rest of the bodies. Would have if Jones hadn't showed up.

"About three more. Keep breathing." Dr. Piel—a woman Maggie judged to be around late thirties, maybe early forties—worked quickly as blood seeped from the four-inch gash. "I'm sorry the topical anesthetic isn't doing anything for you."

"I'd rather feel it." Because it meant she was still alive. That Toledano hadn't gotten his way. Though she could use a few more days before her next abduction. *You can run, but you can't hide.* The masked soldier, the one who seemed to outrank *Sangre por Sangre*'s own beloved heir, was on a mission. He and his unit never broke orders. Never gave up. He'd destroyed the SD card, burned the bodies of the American soldiers she'd witnessed slaughtered. They were ready to kill her and cover up the whole operation. And for what?

Orders. The word seemed to bury deep in her brain, waiting there between every thought. Soldiers like that—like Jones and the rest of Socorro's operatives—went to extreme lengths to complete their assignments. But soldiers thrived in the field. They liked getting their hands dirty. They weren't resigned to shuffle paperwork from behind a desk. The plan had to be handed down. But from whom? *Sangre por Sangre*? Or someone else?

Pain kicked her back into a bright white room so out of place in Socorro's headquarters. The lights were getting to her. The aches were getting to her. The lack of sleep and food and pure confusion were getting to her. Adrenaline only carried a person so far, and Maggie had run out of that a long time ago.

"All done." Dr. Piel tossed the curved needle and surgical thread into a stainless steel bowl on the moveable cart beside her. The physician seemed meticulous, moving with confidence and efficiency. It was easy to imagine how she spent her nights when she wasn't on call here. Most likely with her nose in a nonfiction book and a glass of wine in one hand. Surrounded by expensive upholstery, good art and an entire library at her disposal. Definitely not the kind of woman Maggie would've been friends with in her past life, or even the type who scrolled through Pinterest. "I'm going to wrap a bandage around this to keep you from snagging the stitches on anything. Try to keep it from getting wet and let me know if the pain gets worse. I cleaned it out the best I could, but there's still a chance of infection."

"Thank you." Maggie stared down at the angry red pricks along her opposite arm where glass, rocks and embers from the fire had made their marks. It was nothing compared to the welts and internal damage several days of interrogation had left behind.

"How's the back?" Dr. Piel disposed of her latex gloves in a hazardous materials bin on the other side of the medical suite before she collected her tablet from the counter. "Any changes I should be made aware of?"

Maggie scrunched her toes around the dust that collected inside her shoe from her left leg dragging behind her as she, Gotham and Jones had made a run for the truck mere hours ago. The numbness had spread from her toes, into her ankle, up her calf and now around her knee. She didn't know what that meant. Didn't know how long she had before she lost use of the leg entirely, but it didn't really matter. She'd walked straight into a cover-up that had the potential to change her life if she dug deep enough. And she had to move fast. Things like this came with a deadline. If she was going to be the one to break the news, she couldn't waste another second. And she couldn't let anyone try to stop her. "A little soreness in my lower back, but it's getting better."

"Good. Be sure to keep me updated if that changes." The good doctor made a few notes on her tablet, too distracted to read Maggie's lie straight from her face. "I don't see any other injuries that need immediate attention. Feel free to take ibuprofen as needed, get into a nice hot shower for the muscle aches and sleep as much as you can."

"I will. Thank you." Maggie slid off the examination table, careful to hold her weight in her arms and not her left leg. She'd gotten good at pretending over the years. That her marriage was perfect, that her family and friends hadn't hurt her when they'd taken her ex's side, that she deserved this new life she'd created. Keeping her leg steady as she walked out of Socorro's medical suite was just another version of that.

She headed back into the black corridor, the awareness of being watched instantly pressurizing between her shoulder blades. Not out of fear. Familiarity. Trust. Relief. The knot in her stomach almost released, but Maggie wasn't sure she wanted it to. Because the second she gave up her guard, she put herself at risk. And she'd come too far to take a step back now. "You don't have to follow me around, you know. I'm not sure I could even find the front door if I wanted to leave. This place is a maze."

"What did the doc say?" It took nothing for Jones to catch up to her as she shuffled down the hall.

"Apart from the gash in my arm, everything looks fine." Lie. Her toes caught on a grout line in the black tile, and Maggie forced herself to slow down. To take a breath as her chest tightened. Jones had done nothing but fight for her, to the point of risking his own life and the lives of his team. She owed him the truth about the side effects from whatever Toledano had injected into her spine, but telling him only guaranteed her sitting on the sidelines. Or letting Socorro take control of her life. She wasn't going to let that happen. Not again. "I've been ordered to take a long hot shower and sleep myself into a coma."

"I think I can help with that." Such a simple statement, but one that held so much meaning if she let herself read into it.

Maggie pulled up short of the kitchen. "Are you offering to help me shower?"

"What? No." Pure panic contorted his handsome features as Jones raised both hands in surrender. His palms had been cut up—like hers. A scratch cut through his hairline and came dangerously close to his eye. Scabs would start building in the next day or so, but right now, everything was fresh. There were still streaks of dirt around the wound. He hadn't been to see the doctor. He'd waited outside that room for her. "That's not what I meant. Unless you need my help. Then, yeah. I can do that."

"At ease, soldier. I think I can manage on my own." Her upper lip stung as she found herself smiling. She'd never seen him flustered before. It made him human. Maggie leveraged one hand against the wall as she rounded into the kitchen. As much as she wanted to follow straight through with Dr. Piel's orders, she couldn't do any of it until she had something to eat. Training for her first marathon last year had taught her the body physically couldn't repair itself without the proper macronutrients. She'd feel better faster after a substantial amount of calories. "I needed the laugh, though. Thanks for that."

She could almost feel his hand at her lower back. Just waiting for her to need his help. But the part of her that'd picked herself up off the floor after her divorce wouldn't let her rely on anyone but herself. It was that part that'd given her the courage to leave everything she'd known behind and gotten her the job with *American Military News*. This was who she had to be now.

Morning sun peeked out from behind the canyon walls protecting the small town less than a mile east. What would it be like to live in a place like that? Outside the city, away from the mania and rush. Where neighbors knew each other's names and checked in with homemade goods and smiles. To live slow and without the pressures of trying to keep up with everyone else. Her heart craved that. Or maybe she was just tired. And beat up. And bleeding. Maggie used the galley-style kitchen counters to take her weight as she passed through to the oversize dining table on the other side. "What's for breakfast?"

"I make a mean omelet, if you're interested." Jones moved about the kitchen with a grace she'd never be able to pull off even if she wasn't injured. He grabbed a pan from one cupboard and a cutting board from another before verbally greeting each of his items as he collected them from the refrigerator. "Peppers, onions, eggs, cheese, salt, pepper and my secret ingredient. Our logistics coordinator is something of a chef in her downtime. She's been teaching us to cook in case we have to fend for ourselves."

"Great. I'll take three." She eased herself down onto the nearest chair, giving up her need to put her back to the wall so she could see the entire room. "And I'm not kidding."

"You got it." He dumped his haul on the counter with a little too much force, splitting the bell pepper along the top. "You don't have any allergies, do you?"

The question shouldn't have meant much, but she wasn't sure anyone had ever asked her that before. If they'd ever put her well-being first. Her ex certainly hadn't, and her parents had turned over that responsibility to herself long before she'd left the house at seventeen. "No. I'm good. Don't all of you soldier types know how to fend for yourselves in the field?"

"MREs are not the same as a home-cooked meal." He cracked an entire dozen eggs, one after the other, against the countertop before dropping them into a mixing bowl.

"So there's no one cooking you meals at home? Girlfriend, wife?" She shouldn't have asked. It wasn't any of her business and the answer wouldn't change anything between them. They'd been thrust together for the sake of survival. That was it. There wasn't any version of her story that included getting involved with another man capable of breaking her. And Jones Driscoll had the ability to break her. "Boyfriend?"

"I live here." His smile cracked at one side of his face as he whisked the eggs together and combined them all in a pan to cook along with the cheese before he started dicing vegetables. A gravitational pull suddenly held her pinned to her seat. This wasn't the soldier who'd pulled her out of danger. This was the man beneath the armor. The one who might've existed before his brother's death. And he was giving her, of all people, the gift of seeing it firsthand. "And, no. I don't have a significant other, if that's what you're asking."

Gratitude and raw desire propelled her to her feet. Maggie put everything she had into getting to her feet. Her leg tried to keep up, but she was losing her own determination to hide from him. Stopping mere inches away, she reached for his face, framing his jaw between both hands. "That's too bad."

She dragged his mouth to hers.

A BURST OF adrenaline twisted his stomach tight.

Jones knew this kind of excitement. It was the same feeling he lost himself in when heading into the field for an assignment. There was nothing like throwing himself into a dangerous, chaotic situation, and knowing his life would never be the same when he came back out.

The laceration on Maggie's lip caught against the oversensitive skin of his mouth and rocketed his heart rate into overdrive. It elicited a growl from somewhere deep inside his chest and seemed to urge her on. She parted her lips and gave him access to everything he'd denied himself over the past two years.

Jones let the whisk fall from his hand and speared his fingers into her hair. Bits of dust lodged against her scalp, but that only added to the explosion of sensitivity coiling through his system. Her palms pressed against his chest as though trying to convince herself this was a bad idea, but at the same time giving her the stability she needed to stay upright. And, damn, she tasted perfect. Though he hadn't expected any different over the days they'd been together. He'd known long before this moment she would be an indulgence he'd never be able to get over.

She dug her fingers into his shirt, and it took every ounce of discipline he had not to push her limits. Because no matter how much either of them wanted this, he couldn't give her anything beyond this moment. Despite his desperation for contact that had nothing to do with his work, they were on two separate paths. Him facing down a bloodthirsty cartel with Socorro, and her clawing free of a man who hadn't taken her at her worth. This… This was all there was.

And he'd take it. Every second. Every hour. Every day she'd lend him. He'd soak it all up until he couldn't take any more. He was selfish in that way. He knew that now. Because crossing the lines—breaking orders and risking his entire military career—into enemy territory hadn't been about saving Kincaide from his captors or keeping his brother from suffering more than he had to. That'd been part of it, but Jones realized deep down it'd been about holding on to that single connection for himself. Of not having to lose one more person in his life. Of having someone who gave a damn about him as much as he cared about them. And he cared about Maggie. More than he wanted to admit.

Jones broke away from the kiss, curling his arms around her middle to pull her closer. His mouth found the highjacked pulse at the base of her neck as she tipped her head back.

"Something smells." Her words were breathy. Not entirely coherent. And he couldn't help but love the fact he'd done that to her. That he'd cost her an ounce of that legendary control.

"Sorry about that." Though he wasn't sorry enough to stop. "I haven't showered."

"No. Not that." She set her hands on his shoulders and pushed. "I think your omelet is burning."

The smoke detector's alarm pierced through the pleasant haze and ripped Jones from the edge. He set Maggie back a couple of feet as smoke filled the kitchen. Covering his mouth with the crook of his elbow, he shut off the stove and tossed the mess into the sink as fast as possible. Water scorched the pan and most likely warped the metal, but he'd just have to buy Jocelyn a new one. He grabbed the dish towel hanging from the front of the oven and flapped it in front of the detector to clear a bit of the smoke. The alarm ceased its deafening beeping, and Jones's blood pressure started coming down. "Look what you did."

"Me? You're the one who forgot you were cooking. I'm innocent in all of this." Maggie waved one hand in front of her face. A smile that had no business visiting a moment like this brightened her face and gutted him faster than any blade. She reached for the dining table behind her and took a seat. "But if it makes you feel better, I'll keep my distance. Because I still want eggs."

Jones whipped the dish towel over his shoulder and set about pulling another carton of eggs from the fridge. "Save me from the cartel. Make sure I don't get shot. Help me escape from being burned alive. Cook me eggs. Is there anything else I can do for you, Ms. Caddel?"

"You could do it without a shirt." She leaned back in the chair, completely at ease, and damn, he'd never seen anything so beautiful in his life.

And it was right then he knew. Maggie's life hadn't always revolved around the idea she could change everything by meeting some goal she'd convinced herself would finally make her happy. She'd been in survival mode. Not just running for her life from the cartel over the past few days, but from being the person her ex branded her as to her family and friends. He could see why breaking a story that had the potential to shoot her to the top of her profession would look so tempting. To prove her worth, that she was someone, that she meant something. And Jones wanted to give her that.

"I wouldn't mind," she said.

He set to work cracking another dozen eggs, then whisked them together with the cheese to start a second batch of omelets. That kiss had brought him down to his baser instincts. Going much longer without a full stomach would finish the job. Jones layered a base of eggs in a new pan and let it sit while he started chopping the vegetables. "Why don't you tell me what happened after the accident instead?"

The playfulness drained from her expression, and he hated himself for being the root cause of her anxiety, but if they were going to live up to the deal they'd made at the start of all this, they needed to be honest with each other. That was the agreement. No secrets. No holding back. Maggie cut her gaze to some invisible speck on the table, scratching at it with one finger. "All right. I think the men who took me from the SUV were US military. Active. From what I could gather from the short—and terrifying—conversation I had with the leader of their little party, they were ordered to cover up what happened the night of the ambush."

He'd assumed as much in the mere minute and a half he'd engaged with the unit. Though her theory was new. Jones tossed the vegetables in with the eggs and let everything cook together. Straight up accusing the military of a cover-up wouldn't get them anywhere but a dark hole in which neither of them would escape. They needed proof. "Cover up how?"

"They recovered the SD card with the photos I'd taken. It was right there in front of me. Within reach. I don't know how they found it, but I guess that doesn't matter now. I tried to grab for it, but…" Her voice turned almost wispy, as though she were trying to bury some kind of emotion she didn't want him to see. "The soldier in charge made quick work of destroying it. That and the bodies Toledano burned before you got there. I'm not sure they had any part in that, but from what I could tell they were working together."

"Sosimo Toledano is heir to *Sangre por Sangre*'s entire organization. As soon as his old man kicks the bucket, it's rumored he'll take control. Why the hell would the military or any part of the federal government partner with him?" And why would they cover up the lieutenant's dirty work? Jones was on the verge of letting the eggs burn again. He forced himself to take a minute, to wrap his head around what this all meant.

"That's what I want to find out." She let her hand fall away from whatever she'd tried digging off of the table. "He told me I was the last piece of the puzzle. They were going to kill me, too."

Jones flipped the first omelet, ensuring it was cooked all the way through before slipping it onto a plate with a sprinkle of green onion and his special ingredient: sour cream. He handed it off, his thumb brushing into her palm. "I'm not going to let that happen, Maggie."

And he meant it. No matter what deal they'd struck when they'd gotten into this mess together, he wasn't going to put it ahead of her life. *Sangre por Sangre* wouldn't have to just go through him to get to her. Jones would bring the entire US government down on its head if he had to, and if that didn't work, he'd get her out of the country. Someplace safe. Where she could live the life she deserved.

"I'm not so sure you get a say anymore." Her skin warmed against his for a series of breaths before she pulled the plate to the table. That contact stayed with him as he went back to the stove to start another, tunneling deep into bone. "This is delicious. Who knew someone who communicates in differing levels of growls could cook this well?"

"I think that was a compliment." Jones finished up another omelet and brought it straight to her plate.

"Don't get a swollen head." She stabbed another mouthful of egg and took a bite. Most people might have been grossed out by her ability to talk and eat at the same time, but there was something real and raw about the way she'd opened up to him. About her marriage, her family, her career. His gut said that didn't happen often, if at all. But that maybe she was keeping something else to herself. "It's been over a day since I've had anything—I almost forgot what good food tastes like. For all I know, you're the worst cook in America, and I can't tell the difference."

"I'll take it." A laugh he failed to strangle vibrated

up his throat as he took a seat opposite her. It felt uncomfortable and out of place, foreign, but right at the same time. He'd spent so much of his life trying to be as small as possible—in foster homes, at school, in the military—so as not to gain attention, but with her, he felt…himself. As though he could say or do anything without earning criticism or judgment. Jones reached to grab a bite of omelet from her plate.

She poised her fork above his hand, ready to strike. "I said you're a good cook. Not that I would share. One more move, and you'll never use that hand again."

"Is that a threat?" he asked.

"There's a reason I'm still here." The small muscles in her jaw flexed and released in an attempt to keep her smile under control, but he could see right through her. Had from the beginning. "I won't go down without a fight."

Pure desire tightened his insides. Jones dropped his fork against the table and hauled her against his chest in less time than it took for her to suck in her next breath. "I think I'll take my chances."

Chapter Ten

She was in his bed.

Dark high-end sheets worked to soothe the scrapes, bruises and aches from her body. A hint of his citrus shampoo and conditioner combo filled her lungs as she took in the sunset dipping behind the west mountains through the floor-to-ceiling windows. Maggie let herself lie there, recalling how Jones had carried her back to his room. How he'd started the shower for her—hot as it would go—and left her with fresh towels, toiletries and a pair of sweats and an oversize T-shirt to change into.

She'd taken her time. Not wanting to give up that small amount of peace too quickly. Washed the dirt from her hair, scrubbed her skin raw until the first few layers swirled down the drain. Then conditioned and lotioned while trying to keep the bandage on her arm dry. It was amazing how much a shower could bring back a bit of humanity.

When she'd come back into the main room, she found him changing the sheets. The automatic blackout shades had been drawn, the lights dimmed. He'd looked at her as though she was his whole life right then, and she'd liked it. Felt as though she mattered. That she didn't have to take care of herself. For once, she could let someone else do the job so many others had failed to accomplish. Warmth had started in her belly for the first time in…years. A need that'd triggered when she'd kissed him and hadn't let go. She'd been ready. For him. Ready to move past the loneliness and betrayal she'd gone through with her ex and to start something new.

But Jones had simply wished her good night and left her to sleep the day away.

And in that moment, a shift rocked through her. No. Not a shift. A damn earthquake. She was falling for him. Undeniably, irrevocably falling for a man she intended to use as a source in exchange for providing a layer of protection during this investigation. Jones Driscoll had fought his way into her life and somehow managed to take up space where there shouldn't have been any room left. His loyalty to the people he cared about, how he treated Gotham and fought for his beliefs, had the power to erase the pain she'd insisted on carrying to protect herself. To the point it'd become too heavy around him. And she wanted to leave it behind. Once and for all.

She had that chance. To start over again. Question was, would she take it?

Maggie sat up in the king-size bed and scanned the room she'd been too tired and unfocused to take in this morning. It wasn't as dark as she'd originally estimated. If anything, everything seemed to be in perfect balance between camel-colored leather, dark green paint

and highlights of white in the artwork. Complete with
a few indoor plants. Very boho. A built-in against one
wall took up a good majority of space. Most likely his
closet, given there weren't any other doors other than
the bathroom. She slid from the bed, landing on a faux
fur rug perfectly positioned beneath the frame. Every
inch of this room testified to Jones's attention to detail. Yet somehow it felt…empty. Almost cold despite
the warmth of colors.

Walking the room, she took in everything she could.
No family photos. Not even of his foster brother. Nothing to suggest any hobbies. It was like this place was
merely a way station. A place he intended to pass
through after enough time. Though, Maggie imagined
that'd been intentional. The kind of work he did had
to come with a hazard warning. He wouldn't want to
leave a mess of possessions for someone else to have to
go through. Or maybe it was the result of being moved
from one foster home to the other growing up. At the
same time, he'd painted, hung the artwork and picked
out the furniture. A bundle of opposites.

She skimmed her fingers along the sleek, modern
built-in and pressed one of the doors inward. Mag-
nets. The door swung open, revealing a clean line of
T-shirts and a shelf stacked with folded pants. Everything in its place.

She couldn't help but reach out. Soft fabric warmed
in her hand as she let herself enjoy the sensory input
that couldn't bruise, cut or hurt her. It'd been a long
time since she'd let herself slow down, to just…feel.
There'd been some part of her that was terrified by

the idea. Slowing down meant not moving forward, of being stuck. Of not proving she was better off after the divorce. But the past week, working beside Jones, had shown her she couldn't physically live her life going from one goal to the next without taking a breath in between. And the truth was, she was tired of pushing so hard. Of trying to prove to everyone but herself she was worthy of their love and support. She'd lived these past two years in spite of her ex, unconsciously giving him a power over her he didn't deserve. She'd just wanted to get away, but she'd ended up bringing him along with her.

Maggie brought a T-shirt to her nose and inhaled, long and deep. Making Jones's earthy, clean scent part of her. As though it were enough to keep her safe from what waited outside these bulletproof walls.

"That's not creepy at all," a deep voice said.

Her nervous system spiked in defense. She threw the T-shirt at the source with a pathetic yip as she backed away about a foot. Her heart lodged in her throat as recognition flared. "You scared the crap out of me. How long have you been standing there?"

Jones pulled his T-shirt free of his face and balled it into his hand. "Long enough to thank heavens you haven't gotten to my underwear drawer yet."

Embarrassment heated up her neck and into her face. She didn't know what to say. "For your information, I was… Okay. I was smelling your shirt. I liked the feel of it, and one thing led to another."

"Hey, whatever gets your engine going, I'm all for it." Jones tossed the T-shirt she'd considered smuggling out of the building on to the end of the bed, humor playing at the edges of his eyes. "Thought you might still be asleep. I didn't want to wake you. Doc wanted me to check on you, make sure you were still breathing."

"I'm still breathing." Her arms automatically made an attempt to cross over her midline, as if that would protect her from any further embarrassment on her part. Didn't do any good. Realistically, she didn't have anything to be embarrassed about. At least, that was what she was going to tell herself.

"Searching for anything in particular?" The mattress dipped under Jones's weight as he took position off to her left.

Her throat convulsed. "Not really. Hoping maybe you had a phone or a laptop stashed somewhere in here. It's been a few days since I've touched base with my editor. The last time I talked to him, I came clean about following those *Sangre por Sangre* members. Told him I was going to see this through to the end. I was captured that night. I can't imagine what he's going through not being able to reach me, how many people are looking for me."

"Reaching out could tip *Sangre por Sangre* and whoever the hell else they're working with to your whereabouts." No hint of emotion or surprise. Just statement of fact.

"You and I both know Socorro has ways of masking GPS signals. Otherwise, you wouldn't be able to do your job." Her gut said there was more to his detachment. Maggie stepped closer to him, almost between his knees. "What aren't you telling me?"

His jaw flexed under the pressure of his back teeth. "Your editor isn't looking for you, Maggie. I've been monitoring the police bandwidths and cross-referencing missing person reports. Even had Alpine Valley's chief of police reach out to Albuquerque PD. No one knows you were abducted."

He didn't have to finish the rest of that thought. The last two words were already at the front of her mind. *Or cares.*

"That's…not true." Blood rushed from her upper body and pooled in her thighs. A knot pinched behind her shoulder blade, cutting her next breath short. She had coworkers. Neighbors. Even her ex must've noticed he hadn't been able to torture her for a week. Someone must've realized what'd happened. Someone had to care. A low ringing started in her ears. She wasn't alone. Because if she was, that meant everything she'd done over the past two years had been worthless. That she was worthless. No friends. No family. No one to miss her. That wasn't a life. That was living as a ghost. She stretched out her hand. "Give me a phone."

"I've been monitoring the news for days. Your name hasn't been brought up." His voice leveled, which somehow cut deeper than his initial accusation. "This is a good thing, Maggie. Staying off the radar gives *Sangre por Sangre* a chance to forget about you over time. You can move on. Start fresh, maybe somewhere else. You can leave all of this behind."

"I already started over. I already gave up everything and everyone I loved. I can't just walk away from that." Because the unknown was far more terrifying than the threat she knew. Her hand shook as she waited for him to budge. "Give me a phone."

"This is a mistake." Jones unpocketed his cell, tapped in the passcode and handed it off.

"I don't care." She latched onto the device as though it would solve the problems closing in. She knew better than to trust her emotions. They hadn't done her any good before, but she had to know for herself. Dialing her editor's direct line, she pressed the phone to her ear. The line rang once before connecting. "Bodhi?"

"You got him. Who's this?" he asked.

Her heart squeezed at the fact he hadn't recognized her voice. Which was currently shaking. "It's Maggie."

"Maggie, where the hell are you? You missed your deadline. I had to give your piece to Don. You were already on a short leash, and now you think you can just skip out on me?" The tap of a keyboard cut through his end of the line. "You know what? I don't care. I've got to have something from you by the end of the day or you're gone. Got it?"

The nerves in her temple lit up as she pressed the phone harder to her ear. "Bodhi, you remember what I told you about those *Sangre por Sangre* soldiers? The ones peeling off from their corners?"

"What about it?" A palpable energy shifted as the *tap tap tap* of the keyboard died on the other end of the line. Bodhi lowered his voice. "You got something for me, Mags?"

"I followed them out into the desert." Her skin felt too tight as Jones leveled that gaze on her. Like he could see right through her. "I saw them kill ten American soldiers during an operation to capture Sosimo Toledano. The cartel buried the bodies, then a military unit came along and burned them, but I had proof. I took photos. They abducted and tortured me for them. People need to know, Bodhi. This is big."

There was so much more she needed to tell him, but the excitement of the story was getting to her. Her editor's heavy exhale filled the silence, but he hadn't given her an answer. "So do you think we have something?"

"Where are the photos?" he asked.

Her stomach clenched. It always had to come back to proof. *American Military News* wasn't some tabloid that ran pieces on the promise of getting subscriptions. Journalists had to work through classified intel, establish contacts within the military and walk a thin line between exposing government secrets and doing their jobs. "I don't have them anymore. They were destroyed."

"I didn't want to do this, but now I don't have any choice. You're fired, Maggie." Bodhi's voice sounded sad. And afraid. "Don't contact me or any of the other writers here again. I won't answer."

The line disconnected.

Maggie handed back the phone, her face white, jaw slack. "I need a computer."

Hell. She wasn't going to take the truth at face value. No one had filed a missing person report. No one had gone to the landlord when they couldn't get her to answer the door. No one had attempted to contact her since her abduction. Not a scammer or the bank to ask about the inactivity on her cards, according to her phone records. That feeling—the one trying to convince her she was utterly forgotten and alone—was a lie. She had him. She had Gotham and the rest of the team at Socorro. "Maggie, I know what you're—"

"He fired me." Her eyes glittered with unshed tears. "I told him what I'd uncovered, and he fired me. Said I shouldn't contact him or any of the other writers. Then he hung up."

His instincts prickled as Jones got to his feet. He took back the phone he'd lent her, on high alert. "Why would he fire you?"

"I have no idea." Maggie threaded her hands through her hair, turning away from him. The armor she'd donned against the world was starting to shed. She was coming apart at the seams. "This job…was everything, Jones. It was providing the income I needed to finally live on my own. I'm going to lose my apartment, but worse, I'm going to have to use the money my ex pays in alimony every month to survive and prove him right. That I can't live on my own, that I'll always need him. That I'm nothing without him."

"He told you all those things?" Deep-seated anger filtered through his muscles until his arms and legs ached under the pressure.

"Amongst other things." She swiped the back of one hand against her face. "But I was finally figuring this out for myself. I was…happy. I felt like I belonged there. It was cutthroat, but the pressure to perform was making me better. I wasn't stuck. I had a plan. And now… It's gone." She collapsed onto the bed, her head in her hands. "What am I going to do? No news outlet is going to touch me after this, and you were right. My editor didn't even know I'd been abducted. No one knows, or they don't give a damn, and isn't that just pathetic?"

Jones wanted nothing more than to hunt the bastard down who'd dared step on her confidence and self-worth and show the man the error of his ways—and maybe what a few cracked ribs felt like. But Maggie needed him more at this moment. He dropped to his knees in front of her, setting both hands along her thighs. Lean muscle contracted at his touch, an automatic response honed over the course of permanently living in fight-or-flight mode. "Maggie, look at me."

She didn't move, didn't even seem to breathe.

"Maggie." Something in his voice brought her head up. "The people who believed a narcissistic, manipulative jackass like your ex and turned their backs on you are dicks."

Her laugh jolted her upper body. "That's one way of looking at it."

"You want to know why your friends and family chose his side? Because they were afraid. They thought letting you slip out of their lives would be easier than disproving the lies he told them about you, and they were right." Jones squeezed her leg as an unfamiliar tightness constricted around his rib cage. He wasn't good at this stuff. Empathizing. Showing how much he cared. His entire life had been forged from abandonment and searching for support that might not even exist in his line of work. Of being the first through the door and getting the job done in hopes someone would be proud of him. He was the wrong person to sit here and try to convince Maggie she didn't need to earn her happiness.

"I can't tell you that you're better off without them because we all need those connections. We all need to know that if we fall, someone will be there to catch us. But look at you. You took a stand. You made a life for yourself all on your own. You survived multiple days of interrogation and pain and came out the other side stronger. I know at least one man who wasn't capable of that."

Grief tugged hard at his insides at the thought of Kincaide's last moments, where the effects of brain damage had gotten so bad Kincaide had no longer recognized his own brother. "You're a fighter, Maggie. You see something and you go after it, and I admire the hell out of that. You stood up to an entire unit of soldiers ready to kill you, not to mention put up with me the past few days. That doesn't come close to pathetic in my book."

"I can definitely say putting up with you is a feat in and of itself." Her smile deepened the dimple at the right side of her mouth. Just before it slipped from her face. "But the past week has shown me something. I don't want to be a fighter anymore, Jones. I don't want to be strong or resilient. I don't want to inspire people with my struggles or have my entire self-worth dependent on my job. I'm so tired of fighting." She took his hands in hers. "I want to be soft. And loved. I want to feel safe enough to make mistakes and be normal instead of going from one life trauma to the next. I want to be able to sit on the couch and watch a TV show without feeling guilty for slowing down. I want to be happy."

His throat dried up on his next inhale. She deserved it. She deserved all of it. And, hell, Jones wanted to be the one to give it to her. To make her feel safe and loved and soft. Because maybe he wanted a little bit of that, too. And why couldn't they give that to each other? Her soft skin caught on the callouses along his knuckles.

"But I'm not giving up on this story." Determination bled through the exhaustion playing at the corners of her eyes. "Bodhi might've fired me, but I know there's something big going on here. Somebody ordered that unit to cover up the *Sangre por Sangre* ambush the night I was taken hostage, and I want to know who. I'm owed that much, and I need your help."

"I gave you my word when we got into this mess I would see this through," he said. "And I keep my promises. What do you need?"

"Access to a laptop or computer or a notepad and pen." Maggie shoved herself to standing and started pacing the room. A frenzy of energy burned behind her eyes. Though her left leg seemed to drag slightly behind the right. He hadn't noticed that before. "I need to write down everything that's happened so far so I don't forget any details. About that night, about the military unit destroying evidence and Toledano's involvement. That soldier, the one in charge, he burned my SD card, but we might still be able to recover the photos I took that night if we can get our hands on my camera. Maybe not all of them, considering the limited memory, but there's a chance."

"Slow down. You're talking about the camera *Sangre por Sangre* confiscated when they took you captive?" Jones got to his feet and approached the built-in. Pressing one cabinet corner down, he revealed a safe. The fingerprint reader glowed green, giving him access to the contents inside, and he extracted his laptop. If he didn't give Maggie something to do in the next few seconds, he feared she might explode. "I thought you said it broke when you fell."

"The gunman who found me hiding in the bushes took it from me and handed it over to Toledano. After that, I'm not entirely sure what happened to it." She hadn't stopped pacing, the excitement of a lead clear in her voice. "But even if we have the photos, that doesn't prove who ordered Toledano's capture or who is trying to cover up the deaths of those soldiers. We'll need more. My editor… He sounded scared after I told him what happened. Like he needed to wash his hands of anything having to do with the story. I think he might know something."

"I'll have Alpine Valley PD run a background check on him, review his financials and phone records. He told you not to contact him or anyone at the paper, but if your editor is connected to the cartel in any way, we'll at least have leverage we can approach him with."

Though explaining his continued involvement in all this to Ivy Bardot—despite not finding evidence at the ambush site—had the potential to end his access to

Socorro's internal systems and their partnership with local law enforcement—and end his career.

Hesitation had his thumb gripped over the contact information for Alpine Valley's chief of police. Socorro had given him a second chance after he'd directly disobeyed orders not to go after Kincaide overseas. Ivy and the rest of the team trusted him to do what was best for the company and the people they protected. Going off script—following Maggie to the end of the line and disobeying another set of orders—would put all that at risk. Could cost him everything.

He watched as Maggie took the laptop to the edge of the bed and navigated to a notes app. Within seconds, he'd lost her to a frantic pace of typing. Her mouth silently followed the words she put on the page, and it was easy to see, despite not working for *American Military News* anymore, she had a passion for investigating. For getting to the truth and ensuring the public got the answers they deserved. That she was good at this. Happy, even.

"There's another option." Jones tucked his phone back into his cargo pants pocket without reaching out to the police again. He would. In time. The editor was a good start, but they had the means to cut out the middleman and end this sooner rather than later. Without putting his second chance in danger. "Another source we haven't considered."

"What source?" Maggie pulled herself away from the soft white glow of the screen, setting that newly brightened gaze on him. Understanding sank in the longer she studied him, and a tenseness that'd taken days for her to lose infiltrated her upper body. She dragged herself off the bed. "You've got to be joking. No. No way in hell."

"You and I both know he's the fastest way to get to the truth, Maggie." Though Jones would give anything not to put her in this position. Because he wouldn't have asked it of his brother. He wouldn't have asked it of anyone on his team. But this story was something that could destroy her from the inside if she let it, and they had a chance to finish this once and for all.

"You mean if he's even still alive, which for the record, I hope he is and that he's suffering from the bullet you gave him and being slowly eaten by that fire." She pointed a strong index finger at him. "Toledano kidnapped and tortured me for three days, and now you just want me to walk right up to him and ask, 'Hey, want to tell me about who's trying to cover up your massacre that killed ten American soldiers? Oh, and can I have my camera back? Pretty please?'"

"I'll let you throw a couple punches if it'll make you feel better," he said.

She cut her attention to the laptop and the beginnings of the story she had there. "If you want me to do this, it's going to be more than a couple."

Chapter Eleven

She could do this.

She had to do this.

Maggie held her breath as the compound came into sight up ahead. In truth, she didn't remember a whole lot about the outside. The *Sangre por Sangre* soldiers who'd taken her the night of the operation to capture Toledano had dragged her inside unconscious. The first thing she'd remembered was waking up in the dark, dank hole she'd come to treasure between interrogations.

She would've done anything to escape this place. Now she was going back into it willingly. But Jones had been right. The fastest way to get answers was by questioning the source. Though she couldn't imagine why Bodhi had opted to fire her instead of chasing a story of this caliber. The answer to that question would have to wait, but the betrayal refused to let up.

She'd had no illusions *American Military News* would be a career home forever. It'd been meant as a stepping stone, one that'd helped her land on her feet after the divorce. Support her long enough to get a place of her own and build a reputation in the media world.

Before her marriage had imploded, she'd cut her

teeth on articles here and there in tandem with her day job as a freelance copywriter for a variety of different companies. Her husband hadn't wanted her to work at all, hoping to convince her to start a family before she lost all her eggs to age. But it'd been her own little private investigation into a case of a missing naval officer she'd read about in the papers that ended in him being found. She spent her nights watching true crime and gobbling up every book she could get her hands on. It was the investigations—of one clue leading to the next, of reliving the journalist's setbacks and triumphs, that propelled her to give it a try. The naval officer's aunt had been calling for any information, offering a reward, but something had seemed off. The aunt's insistence he would be okay—that he was strong and resourceful and a fighter—had Maggie watching the aunt's home for a couple days. There hadn't been any sign of the officer between news outlet campouts, but she'd noticed an uptick in groceries. More than a woman of his aunt's size would need. She'd marched straight up to the door during one of the "please find him" interviews and exposed him as a coward hiding in his bedroom. The resulting attention had given her a base to apply for the war correspondent position.

But while she'd ultimately taken the job to help dig her out of what was left of that old life, there was a mass of emptiness in her chest at its loss. She'd thought she was doing something she was good at for once. Subscriptions had been up, with spikes every time Bodhi had published one of her pieces. The people of New Mexico found it more important than ever to keep an eye on the war between the federal government and *Sangre por Sangre* after what'd happened in Alpine Valley about a month ago. Because any one of their towns could be next. She'd been a part of that. Made a difference. And now…

Now she didn't know what she was supposed to do.

"You two sure know how to make a girl's day." Scarlett Beam turned her gaze out the driver's side back window as they shot across the desert, one hand set on a Doberman she'd called Hans. The other one, Gruber, prodded Gotham in the face with his nose. "It's been weeks since I've taken on a good assignment. You can only run diagnostics on security equipment so many times before you start imagining threats. Except for the part where one of my teammates brings home a journalist who starts unplugging my cameras."

Heat flared into Maggie's face. Bits and pieces of memory broke into the moment. She'd done that. Right after she'd woken up in the medical suite that first time. She hadn't thought much about it at the time. Especially that someone would've had to go back and fix what she'd done. "Sorry about that. I hope I didn't damage your equipment."

"I would've done the same thing in your position." Scarlett scratched the nearest Doberman, but there was something in that statement that hinted at a similar experience. One where the woman in the back seat might've had to face her own survival.

"Unofficial assignment." Jones cut his gaze into the rearview mirror. "We clear?"

"We're clear. I honor my deals, Driscoll." The security consultant nodded. "I won't tell Ivy about today's little field trip and that you have nothing to support your cover-up theory, and you won't rat me out for... my little indiscretion you walked in on."

Silence bubbled between the three of them. Maggie forced herself to stare out the windshield. The chain-link fence surrounding the compound glinted under the hot desert sun ahead. The curiosity embedded deep in her soul and that'd urged her to apply as a journalist in the first place built to the point Maggie couldn't help but turn in her seat. Finding out why people did what they did. That was the basis of a good investigative reporter and war correspondent. If she bothered to slow down and let herself think about it, that was why she'd applied to the magazine in the first place. To understand what type of person, who'd claimed he was willing to stick with her until the end, suddenly felt the need to destroy her from the inside. "What did you—"

"She smuggled in a guy she was sleeping with without clearing it through Ivy first." Jones fought the slight rise at one corner of his mouth. "Which doesn't sound as bad as it should. Except we have security protocols every operative swears to live by when they sign on to work for Socorro. We can't risk outsiders coming across our data or accessing our systems and files."

"The best people to get around security protocols are the ones who built them in the first place." Vibrant red hair alluded to the fiery personality armored beneath her own Kevlar vest and protected by more weapons than Maggie could count. But Maggie had never counted on stereotypes. Data. Behavior. Connections.

Those were the categories that defined a person. Not their hair color. But from what Maggie could see, Scarlett Beam wasn't the type of person to roll with the punches. She was ready for any possibility and planned every detail accordingly. Probably liked to stick to a routine, stubborn about change. No, not stubborn. Terrified. Maggie imagined a security consultant like her didn't care for surprises in her work or personal life. And she most certainly hadn't planned on Jones.

Funny. Neither had Maggie.

"Let's just say I did my own background check on him." Scarlet winked. "It was very thorough."

"We're here." Jones let the SUV roll to a stop before shoving the transmission into Park, and suddenly, the lightness they'd created in such a small amount of time evaporated, leaving Maggie heavier than when they'd decided on this plan. "Satellite footage isn't giving us any activity here in the past twenty-four hours. That's the only reason I agreed to this, but you know the deal. Scarlett and I will surveil the perimeter before heading inside. I'll give you the all clear if we deem it safe enough. If we come into contact with Sosimo Toledano, we'll secure him and his men before we question him."

He studied her for a beat, and Maggie knew exactly what he was going to say before the words left his mouth. That was what happened when relationships were honed from a biological need to survive. A connection—stronger and deeper than anything she'd experienced—had forged between them since that terrible night. As though he felt every twinge, every nodule of doubt in her body, and she in his. Jones didn't want to do this. He didn't want her to have to come back here. He didn't want to risk her well-being to prove there was something to their theory. But it was the only way. They both knew that. "You don't have to face him."

"I suddenly feel the need to not be here. Hans, Gruber." Scarlett clicked her tongue to call the Dobermans, and Gotham's whine at losing his friends filled the SUV's cabin. The security consultant slammed the door behind her.

Spearing his fingers around her ear and into her hair, Jones brought Maggie's forehead to his over the center console. "We can come at this another way. Take a shot at your editor. See what he knows and why he killed the story."

She wanted that. More than anything. To get away from here. To forget what she'd been through and wipe it clean from every angle of her life. It was the shame that hurt the most. The fact that she'd failed to protect herself, that she hadn't seen the threat coming at all. That she'd let another man beat her at her own game.

Maggie set her hand over his, borrowing his strength. Just a little bit. That was all she needed. Him. She closed her eyes, memorizing this moment, feeling him against her skin. She'd never done that with another man, even while she'd been with her ex. Because on a cellular level, some part of her hadn't trusted him, feared what he'd do if she took her eyes off him. But she trusted Jones. From the very beginning, he'd fought for her. Sacrificed for her. Defended her to the very end. Data. Behavior. Connections. His told a story of loyalty and support and love, and that there didn't seem to be anything that could break him. Least of all her. He was everything she'd wanted for herself. He was everything she deserved. "No. You were right before. Questioning Sosimo Toledano is the smart move. And I need to do this, Jones. Otherwise, that fear is going to control me for the rest of my life, and I've already lost too much time to men like him."

"Okay." He extracted his hand from her hair and reached for the door handle. A gust of hot wind intensified the heat he'd curated along her neck and head as his boots hit the ground. "I'm coming back for you, Maggie Caddel."

"I know." Not a lie. The SUV shook as he secured her inside. Visually following him through the windshield, Maggie admired the grace both operatives somehow managed with over thirty pounds of gear and weaponry. The Dobermans fanned out ahead of their handler but soon vanished beneath the rim of the man-made crater protecting *Sangre por Sangre*'s abandoned headquarters below.

She reached for the radio pinned to the dashboard, the plastic frame protesting under her grip. One minute. Then five. No word yet. The sun cut through the windshield and spiked her internal body temperature. Sweat built up at her temples as her heart rate climbed higher. No signs of gunshots or an alarm. Not even a bark from the Dobermans. Was this supposed to be a no-news-is-good-news operation?

Gotham threaded his front paws over the center console and wormed his way into the driver's seat. Lengthening his neck, he studied the landscape through the window, then turned those iridescent blue eyes on her for answers.

"I know how you feel." Maggie scruffed the fur along his back, which obviously meant she wanted him in her lap because suddenly the husky's butt landed on top of her thigh. She couldn't fault him for needing a bit of assurance. She needed it, too. "It'll all be okay. Jones and Scarlett know what they're doing."

Static crackled through the radio, and Maggie brought it to her ear. She needed something—anything—to feed that panicked part of herself ready to bolt from the SUV and follow after them.

"We found him. Toledano and his men." Jones's voice tensed every muscle down her spine as seconds distorted into agonizing silence. "But we're not going to get answers here. They're all dead."

THEY'D BEEN TOO LATE.

The bodies were cold. Dead for more than a day based off the smell.

"Ambush." Scarlett Beam wove between the corpses, her mouth buried in the crook of her elbow. She bent down to collect a container of some sort as Maggie stood at the peripheral of the scene. Gotham was going nuts, signaling each time he encountered another set of remains. "Food wrappers, empty water bottles, burn ointment. I'd say Sosimo Toledano and his men were hiding out after what went down at the arch two nights ago. I doubt they cut their own power though.

I'm guessing the team who surprised them yesterday did that."

She was right. Jones grazed his flashlight beam over the walls. Blood mixed in with cinderblock, water and bullet holes. Setting the end of the flashlight between his teeth, he pulled the blade from his ankle holster and dug at one of the holes. The projectile popped free as the rotting cinderblock crumpled to the floor, and he dropped the flashlight into his hand. "Three different calibers. Five targets, most likely three separate shooters. Wouldn't have taken them more than a couple minutes to finish the job once they penetrated the perimeter."

His gut clenched as the picture became clear. Jones followed the trajectory of the bullets to the source, the end of the corridor they'd come down. "My guess is they used the garage as an access point. Same as we did. If you had a layout of the place before we blew it to hell the last time, they would've seen that was the best entry point." He tossed the bullet to Scarlett, which she caught against her vest. "Maggie and I met a team capable of this. Seven-man team, all highly trained and determined to tie up loose ends."

The military unit ordered to kill her.

Gotham went from one body to the next, turning in circles. The smell had to be driving him crazy.

"But why? Why leave them here? Why kill them at all?" Maggie's voice… It gripped him until he swore his heart stopped pumping blood. There was something hurried in the tone that worked to counteract the calmness in his. As though she were an emotional regulator for him, and when he thought back, he could see where that was true. How she seemed to bring him down on a logical level when none of this had made sense. Maggie kept her distance from the mass of bodies left to rot away with the rest of the structure. "Toledano was there that night. He helped those gunmen get rid of the bodies from the ambush. They were clearly working together. Why would they kill him?"

"Whoever did this wanted to make sure Sosimo Toledano didn't walk away with their secrets. Or maybe his usefulness just ran out." Scarlett crouched beside the leader's bloated corpse but didn't move to touch anything that might upset the scene. "You said those soldiers were US military, most likely army. As much as it pains me to consider the country I put my life on the line for would step into a deal with people like this, I can't deny your story makes sense now that I've seen evidence for myself." The security consultant watched as her twin Dobermans circled the other side of the room. "I've still got an enlisted contact. Let me reach out, see what I can put together."

"I don't want your name on any requisition forms." That was the only way this was going to work. Scarlett had worked too damn hard for too damn long to put distance between her and the people she'd once trusted to get wrapped up in anything army-related now, and he sure as hell wasn't going to be the one to upset the slice of peace she'd found with Socorro. "Everything stays off the books. You got me?"

"Understood." Scarlett whistled low for her companions, and the Dobermans obeyed without hesitation.

"I'm going to get the lay of the rest of the building. See if I can pick up anything that gives us an idea of who's behind this. Meet you back at the car."

"I'll call this in. Make sure these bodies end up in the right hands." Jones pulled his cell and sent a ping to Chief of Police Baker Halsey. The deaths hadn't occurred within Alpine Valley boundaries, but he was the only man in the department Jones trusted. Halsey would know what to do and who to reach out to. Most likely with Socorro's logistics coordinator—Jocelyn Carville—running point. "Whoever did this wanted to make sure Sosimo Toledano and his men weren't found, and I'm pretty much up for anything to disrupt their plans."

Maggie didn't respond, her gaze locked on the face of her torturer. "It doesn't even look like him."

"Decomposition eliminates a lot of features." Jones didn't really want to get into the specifics. No one should have to witness the slaughter of a human being. No matter how much hatred existed for the deceased. "The medical examiner will have to compare DNA, fingerprints and dental records to get a positive ID."

"No. I know that." Her tongue shot across her lips as she dared a step closer to the body. "I mean, I memorized every centimeter of this man's face while he was interrogating me. I've seen it so many times when I close my eyes, I was sure I'd never forget the small details. But this… This doesn't feel like him."

"It's going to take some time for you to adjust to the idea you don't have to be scared of him anymore," he said.

"You're probably right." She backed away from the body, seemingly realizing how close she'd gotten in the first place. There weren't many civilians willing to confront their greatest fears—especially those in the form of a torturer or person who'd hurt them—but Maggie continued to keep him off balance. She was stronger than she gave herself credit for, but that strength had only come from surviving what most people didn't. His brother included. And, hell, he didn't blame her for wanting a break from it all. To be soft, as she'd put it. Happy. "So the one source we had any chance of getting answers out of is dead. Our only other option is going to my editor. Hoping he knows something."

"I don't make moves based on hope." Jones surveyed the bodies a second time, studying each one after the other. He moved in order of closest to farthest, ending with Sosimo Toledano. "Bullets don't come with serial numbers. The only way we'll be able to trace these are if their striations matched something already registered in the state or federal database, and I doubt these guys would risk using anything to connect back to them or the army. Problem is, we still don't know if they're the ones who made this mess. If they are, it means they would've had to supplement their arsenal. But just like switching from one instrument to another, getting used to a weapon takes time. A couple days at least."

Jones crouched beside Toledano. He targeted a spread of blood in the lieutenant's side. A parting gift of that night at the bonfire. Wrinkled, angry skin contorted the bastard's face and along his left arm. On top of that, a bullet had gone straight through the lower section of his left lung, drowning him from the inside. And hell, Jones wasn't the least bit remorseful of the bastard's final minutes after everything he'd done to Maggie. "They didn't plan on us coming here. Could work in our favor."

"You think the soldiers might not have cleaned up as well as they would have if these bodies were meant to be found. Like they might've left behind prints or maybe some of this blood belongs to one of them if Sosimo Toledano got a shot off." Damn, he loved the way her brain worked. How she almost seemed to read his thoughts and put the puzzle together ahead of him. Maggie shifted her weight between both feet. "How long until your contact in Alpine Valley PD can sort this out?"

No. That wasn't the question she was asking. She wanted to know how much time she had left. How long it would take for the group sent to kill her to finish what they'd started out there at the arch. He shoved himself to his feet. The smell was getting to him. The heat, combined with the lack of air conditioning in an underground basement, only made matters worse. "Processing the scene? Couple hours as soon as they arrive. Getting any kind of result on DNA or prints? Weeks. Every piece of evidence they collect goes through a specialized lab out of Albuquerque. The chief can order a rush, but no one is going to care much about a bunch of dead cartel members."

Silence spread between them.

"I know some people who would care." Her voice barely reached through the darkness.

"What do you mean?" he asked.

"The articles I wrote about *Sangre por Sangre* and what the DEA, the military, even towns across the state were doing in response increased the magazine's subscriptions. Every time." That frenzy, the one he'd noted back in his room, started burning in her eyes in the glow of his flashlight. Her excitement was almost contagious, rocketing his pulse into higher territory. "Once all that business about Alpine Valley hit the news, the public grew obsessed. They couldn't get enough. It was in every paper, on every news site. You couldn't look anywhere without seeing some anchor covering the story. It's a classic universal fantasy. A small town stands up to a drug cartel and comes out on top. Who wouldn't read that?"

"You think this is about media ratings?" He didn't understand. "I wouldn't count a quarter of a town being buried during a landslide set off by an explosive meant to kill the chief of police and one of my teammates as a fantasy."

"No. I'm saying this is about perception." Maggie closed the distance between them. "What if the operation to apprehend Toledano was supposed to end with casualties? He's a high-level target whose capture would make a big impact on *Sangre por Sangre* operations if successful. Given the right kind of intel, it wouldn't be hard to get a mission like that approved. But something goes wrong. Soldiers end up dead."

His gut said she was onto something.

"All right. Let's play this out. *Sangre por Sangre* is accused of killing American soldiers. The media gets ahold of the story. The public is in a rage, most likely calling for action." His brain couldn't help but jump to his employer. Socorro's contract with the Pentagon was binding until the next review in a week, but there hadn't been a shortage of outrage from towns in the vicinity at having a private military contractor setting up shop close by. Outrage from local government officials, too. There was one in particular... Jones couldn't think of his name. A senator who'd been calling for the Pentagon to revoke contracts with private military outfits like Socorro's. Jones tried to force the pieces to fit into the puzzle they'd stumbled into. He pointed to the cartel members at his feet. "But good news. The US military has taken down the bad guys responsible."

"Except units like the one we came across don't issue their own orders." Maggie slipped her hand up his forearm as the truth gutted him from the inside.

"They follow them." Jones tried to breathe through the acid burning up his throat. "Someone higher up sent those soldiers to die."

"Only I wasn't supposed to be there." She scanned the bodies. "And they're trying to kill me to cover it up."

Chapter Twelve

They still didn't have any proof.

Jones and Scarlett had searched the entire compound. There hadn't been any sign of her camera. Their theory was just that. A story that fit, but no one was going to buy it unless they pinpointed the source of the kill order at the top.

And she was beginning to think there was only one way to identify them.

Maggie scrolled through the photos loaded to Jones's laptop they'd taken at the scene before calling in Alpine Valley's police department, once again caught off guard by the swollen face of her torturer. She didn't feel anything. Wasn't she supposed to be relieved? Knowing the man who'd interrogated her—hurt her—wouldn't appear over her shoulder had to come with some kind of pressure release, right? She deserved that much after everything that'd happened. Yet all she felt was emptiness. This feeling that no matter what she did, she couldn't make a damn bit of difference.

It'd been the same after her divorce. Trying to convince her family they'd been gaslighted and manipulated while on the receiving end of accusations of being at fault had led nowhere. And this… This was just like that.

She'd lost her job, her credibility, her support system. She'd suffered trauma and been left with a numbness climbing up into her lower back she didn't know how to stop. No one was going to believe her. Not without the photos she'd taken or eyewitness accounts of the five dead cartel members rotting away in that basement. Any evidence police recovered from now on would support the story ready to be fed to the public. Only she knew the truth.

And she was going to make sure it got out.

Maggie switched back to the document she'd created cataloging the events of the past week. From the moment she'd identified a low-level *Sangre por Sangre* member on a street corner in Albuquerque a year ago to finding Sosimo Toledano and his men dead inside their own compound. So much had happened in between, things she wanted to make sure she didn't forget. Because it was all she would have left once this was over. Cartels like this didn't die when one head was severed from the body. Two replaced the loss until something came along and went for the heart.

Jones slid a steaming mug of coffee across the built-in desk, and the fumes instantly urged her brain into all-nighter mode. "You've been writing for the past four hours without taking a break. Figured you'd need a pick-me-up."

"There are still a few details to work out. Motive, for one. Identifying who marched those soldiers to their deaths, too. I just don't want to mess it up." She cradled the mug between both hands and inhaled the sharp scent of robust beans, cream and sugar. "I can't tell you how much I needed this. Thank you."

She liked this. Him bringing her coffee. Her taking breaks to chat with someone who wasn't trying to steal her job. She even enjoyed the fur ball groaning in his sleep from the dog bed in the corner. It was almost as though they'd slipped into a relationship without ever having really talked about it. Like they fit in a way she hadn't fit with anyone since her divorce. "How much trouble are you in?"

His meeting with Ivy Bardot clung to the tenseness in his shoulders. Jones lowered himself down onto the edge of the bed, his knee brushing against hers. Only he didn't move to avoid her, which she appreciated. Warmth, stability, strength—he was all of that and more. Right when she'd needed it. "I've been ordered to back down from this investigation."

"What does that mean?" The muscles along her spine tightened one by one as she leaned forward to meet him. The answer was already in his expression. He'd warned her about this. About getting in too deep and putting Socorro and what they did here at risk. It was a chance he hadn't been willing to take. With good reason. Understanding settled into her grip around the mug, and Maggie forced herself to set it down on the desk. "You've been ordered to take me back to Albuquerque."

Voicing the words sucker punched her harder than she expected. This past week—the meals together, the kiss they'd shared, the way he'd made her laugh—

they'd meant something. They'd given her hope she didn't have to suffer through the rest of this life unwanted and blamed. That she could mean something to someone again. And now he was going to leave her to fight this battle alone? "I don't understand. You and Scarlett saw the bodies in the compound. We have photos of the scene. You saved me from the unit that was about to kill me. You told the police where to find the victims and the SD card that were burned. It's not like we don't have anything to show. This is all evidence."

"You're right, Maggie, and I wish there was something I could do to change management's mind." His voice leveled as though he was talking to a complete stranger. Not a woman he'd partnered with, kissed, made dinner for and given his bedroom to so she could recover from a brutal attack. "But Scarlett reached out to her contact in the army. The second she asked about the classified operation to apprehend Sosimo Toledano, the army arrested her and threatened Socorro's contract with the Pentagon."

She couldn't sit still anymore, shoving herself to her feet. Her head was spinning. All the dominos they'd stood on end were starting to fall out of their control. "No. They can't do that. Private military contractors are separate from active military. They have no jurisdiction when it comes to—"

"Unfortunately, they can. Scarlett is not even a year out of discharge, which puts her well within military reach, and Socorro works for the federal government, Maggie. We follow a set of rules and we don't deviate from them, and interfering with a military operation—

warranted or not—is a felony no one comes back from.
We're working to get Scarlett out of custody while Ivy
runs interference. With any luck, we'll still have jobs
at the end of this." He cradled his mug between both
hands, leveraging his elbows against his knees. "I knew
what I was doing when I made the choice to see this
through, but it was my career I was willing to put on
the line. Not that of my team. I'm supposed to take you
back to your place in Albuquerque. Within the hour."

Her blood iced in her veins. He intended to follow
through. She could hear it in his voice, the way he refused to meet her gaze. Maggie shifted her weight onto
her good leg, trying to take some of the pressure off, but
there was nowhere else for it to go. "And do you think
taking me back to a place where that unit can find me
is the best option?"

"You're not staying." Jones got to his feet, his coffee
forgotten. "I can get you a new identity with a passport,
a sizeable chunk of cash and a new phone. It won't be
much, but it will get you out of the country. What you
do after that is up to you, but I recommend finding a
new career. You'll have to avoid anything that can hint
at the life you had here."

"You want me to drop all of this and run?" She motioned to the laptop. "After everything we've uncovered, you're okay walking away and letting whoever
did this get away with the deaths of those soldiers?"

"I don't have a choice," he said. "Not if I want to
keep the life I've built here."

"Yes, you do. You're just afraid to make it. I understand disobeying orders is what lost you your military

career in the first place, but if you hadn't gone after your brother, he would've died in that cave, Jones. You never would've gotten the time with him that you did." Couldn't he see that? Couldn't he see there were some things worth breaking the rules for? "You asked me to trust you, and I have. You made the decision once before. Why can't you do it this time? For me?"

He didn't even flinch under her accusation. Didn't answer. And in that moment, Maggie realized what a colossal mistake she'd made. That she'd fallen for a man she'd thought had seen something worthwhile in her. But the truth was, he only valued the people who had something to give him in return. Who had a use. All she'd offered him was a hail of bullets, five dead bodies and a theory they couldn't prove. She wasn't family or someone he relied on to have his back in the field. She wasn't anything.

Maggie swallowed to counter the tears burning in her eyes. He'd systematically destroyed the armor she'd built to save her from breaking for Toledano, and a rush of heat flared over her neck and face. Damn it. She needed to get out of here. She turned back to the laptop and emailed a copy of the article to everyone in her contacts list. She didn't have anything else. "Don't bother with the cash or the phone or the new identity. I've built a new life before on my own. I can do it again."

"Maggie, don't do this." Jones dared a step toward her but stopped as she turned on him. "The moment you step foot back in Albuquerque, they'll know. They've been watching your apartment, monitoring your financials and phone. Most likely watching your friends and family in case you reach out, too. They will kill you, and everything you've survived will have been for nothing. Please. Let me help you."

Doubt crept in through the heartbreak. All she had to do was slow down and think this through, but her heart didn't want to see logic. It only felt betrayal. And now that betrayal had a new face. "Aren't you worried you'll lose your job?"

Maggie wrenched the door open without looking back. She'd taken careful mental notes on navigating the maze of black corridors over the past few days and found the elevator. Stabbing the descend button as many times as she could without breaking her thumb, she dropped out onto the main floor and walked straight out the front door.

Her heart constricted tight in her chest with every foot she added between her and Socorro's headquarters. But she wasn't going back.

A line of dirt kicked up ahead as a dark SUV raced along the desert floor. It pulled to a stop a few feet away, and the driver's side window lowered to reveal Scarlett Beam, free from military custody. "I take it you're not lost. Need a ride?"

Maggie fought the urge to look back as she rounded the hood of the SUV and climbed into the passenger side seat.

"Where to?" Scarlett asked.

She stared out at the bare landscape capable of eroding even the strongest of mountains. She had to be stronger for what came next. "I'm going home."

HE'D SCREWED THIS up without even trying.

Jones watched from his bedroom window as the SUV flipped around and sped off toward civilization with Maggie inside. She was stubborn enough to walk the entire way back to Albuquerque, but he was grateful she didn't have to. His phone pinged with an incoming message. One tap revealed Chief Baker Halsey's attachment. A police report from a nearby department. He read through the document. "Damn it all to hell."

Maggie didn't have a chance out there on her own. The military unit ordered to clean up after the *Sangre por Sangre* massacre would catch up to her. They'd ensure she never said a word about any of this, and the truth would die with her.

His hands were tied. He'd had a choice. Pursue this investigation to the end of the line with Maggie and risk everything he and the rest of the operatives here at Socorro had built. Or finish the job the Pentagon had contracted them to do: dismantle *Sangre por Sangre* and protect the people of this region. Ivy Bardot had made the stakes clear to him at the beginning.

"Nah. This isn't finished." Jones whistled low to wake Gotham. The husky shot to his feet and followed close on Jones's heels as they navigated through the building and up to the fourth floor. He didn't bother knocking this time, shoving the door to Ivy Bardot's office open. "We need to talk."

Socorro's founder cut her sharp gaze to him. Though there wasn't a single ounce of annoyance as she excused herself from her current phone call and hung up. "I wasn't aware we had another meeting scheduled."

"We don't." His heart refused to drop out of his throat. He'd disobeyed orders before, and it'd cost him his career. Loyalty was what kept him and the rest of his team alive. They had to trust each other in every regard, each a vital cog in the machine that ensured cartels like *Sangre por Sangre* were kept in check. Because the second they lost sight of Socorro's goal, every one of them would fail. But Maggie had been right. If he hadn't disobeyed his orders while at the tail end of his service, he would've lost those precious months he'd gained with his brother. Kincaide would've died at the hands of his captors, buried in an unmarked grave in the middle of the desert. Never to be found. He couldn't stomach the thought of something like that happening to Maggie. "I'm here to tell you that you made the wrong choice about Maggie Caddel."

Hesitation slowed Ivy from restacking a set of documents on her oversize desk. Amusement scratched at the surface of her expression but nothing more. Socorro's founder was out of touch. Safe up here in her ivory tower, where she didn't have to get her hands dirty anymore and operatives did her bidding. Where she didn't have to see the violence and hurt they exacted on her behalf every day. He'd told himself over and over that wasn't the case, but when it came to Maggie, he wasn't so sure anymore. Ivy leaned back in her seat, interlacing her fingers in front of her. "Okay. Enlighten me."

This was his chance. To do what he should've done a long time ago. Save the person he loved. Jones took a step forward and offered her his phone. "Alpine Valley PD ran the ballistics on the bullets found in our friend Sosimo Toledano and his men from that basement. Apart from my bullet, one set came from an XM7 rifle, another from an XM250 automatic rifle and the third from a pistol. All part of the military's move forward with the Next Generation Squad Program proposed by Sig Sauer."

"Military hardware. We don't see a lot of that. At least not new weaponry." Ivy reviewed the report. "You believe this was done by the same team you claim destroyed proof of the operation to capture Toledano the night of Ms. Caddel's abduction and burned the bodies of the soldiers caught in that ambush?"

"I have a hard time believing they're not part of this. Or that they're working rogue, but the order would've had to come down from on high. Someone who has a close relationship with the army, possibly even served and has a couple friends to call in a favor from." Jones was starting to feel that same frenzy, the one Maggie lost herself in when on the cusp of another piece of the puzzle falling into place. It started in his fingers until he grasped the back of one chair positioned in front of Ivy's desk. "Who in the state senate had been calling for us to stand down since we got here?"

A tightness Jones had never witnessed in Ivy flexed the muscles at her jaw as she handed back his phone. "Senator Hawkes. Former army captain. Served his twenty before stepping into the political arena. The man considers *Sangre por Sangre* and organizations like it one of the biggest threats to the state with the amount of drugs they pump into our cities and schools."

"Why the hell would he have anything against Socorro?" he asked.

"Regulations." Ivy sat forward, her elbows on the edge of the desk. "He's managed to get himself on the contract review committee for the Pentagon. He's tried to have our contract terminated every year, insists that despite our military origins, the regulations and laws that apply to the army, navy, marines and air force don't apply to private military contractors as it's spelled out in the agreement. That we're in the business of making money, not protecting this country, and that's why we've let *Sangre por Sangre* spread like a virus through the state."

"He blames us for the cartel's growth," he said.

"Accused Socorro and me of working for our own interests last time I was called in front of the committee. Got quite the support, too. Only not enough to terminate our contract. He's still working on it though. One of these days he just might get what he needs." She dropped her hands open as though that was nothing more than a bridge to cross in the future. "And he's right, in a way. As long as there is a threat from the cartels, we have jobs."

"Whereas the army wouldn't be under the same expectation." He tried to loosen his grip on the back of the chair, but the adrenaline had already taken hold. "That's our motive. What better way to undercut Socorro than to have the army step in and save the day after the cartel is connected to the deaths of ten American soldiers. Show we're not doing enough. That we're not needed, and the army would be much better suited for this job. When is the Pentagon review committee meeting next?"

"In a week." Ivy seemed to consider his words for a series of breaths. "It's clever. I'll give you that, but you have nothing more than an eyewitness who's been through an abduction she didn't report to police, and a ballistics report that Sosimo Toledano and his men were shot with military-grade bullets that could've come from anywhere with enough effort. Even if you had the photos Ms. Caddel claimed she took that night, you don't have the evidence to accuse a state senator of misuse of power, let alone corruption."

"What if I could get it?" Jones had already made his decision. No matter what Ivy said, he wasn't going to sit here and wait for Chief Halsey to forward him the news of Maggie's body showing up in the middle of the desert. "Maggie's on her way back to Albuquerque. The unit sent to cover up all these loose ends is going to come for her. They can't afford to leave her alive. I want to be there when they make their move."

"You want to apprehend and flip one of their soldiers to prove a connection to the senator," Ivy said. "What makes you think they'll talk? Based on what I've seen of their handiwork, these aren't the type of men to negotiate. Their entire lives revolve around orders, and you're not exactly on their Christmas card list."

"I don't know," Jones said. "All I know is I can't leave Maggie to face this alone. She deserves better than that. She deserves to have someone finally keep their word."

"You like her." Socorro's founder stood, rounding her

desk. Ivy cracked her pinkie finger knuckle with one thumb. A tell he hadn't noticed until now. She knew she couldn't stop him, and the lack of control was getting to her. Crossing her arms over her frame, she leaned back against the solid wood. "I can tell you to keep your emotions out of this, but I doubt you're going to listen. Even after what I've seen, some part of me still thinks our emotions are what make us the team we are. I'm not willing to put that to the test, but take it from me, Jones. The only way any of us get out of this is if we trust ourselves. Can you tell me, without hesitation, that you truly believe this is the right course of action?"

Jones evened out his weight between both legs. Surer of himself than ever before. "It's the only course of action, ma'am."

"All right, then. Take your K9 and a partner. Preferably Scarlett as she's been through all this with you up until now," she said. "And, please, for the love of all that is holy, keep this out of the news. We don't need to give Senator Hawkes more ammunition to shoot us with if you fail."

"Understood." Jones was on the move. Excitement for the upcoming fight burned in his veins, drove him harder. He unpocketed his phone and hit Scarlett Beam's contact information as he rounded into his room. The line rang once. Twice. Three times. Nervous energy skittered down his spine as he checked the screen for a good connection. Full bars and Wi-Fi. Pressing the pad of his thumb to the safe's keypad, he listened for the familiar click from the other end of the line.

Only it never came.

The line disconnected, and he tried again.

Gotham groaned as he hiked himself up the floor-to-ceiling window with his front paws. As though he wanted to go after Maggie himself. Jones knew the feeling. It'd been Scarlett's SUV he'd watched Maggie climb into. He was sure of it. The security consultant wouldn't give him the silent treatment in the middle of an assignment like this, even if he was at fault for her arrest.

The call connected.

"Jones…" Scarlett's voice scratched through from the other end of the line, out of breath, wheezy. "It happened so fast. I couldn't stop them. She's gone. Maggie is gone."

Chapter Thirteen

"Do you know who I am?" an unfamiliar voice asked.

Maggie tried to drag her chin away from her chest, but it hurt. Everything hurt. Her head slipped back, hitting something solid. Pain lightninged across her skull and into her face. Like she'd been hit straight on by a train. She knew this feeling—hated it—and suddenly she was right back in that room. Waiting for El Capitan's next round of questioning. Her throat worked to come up with the answer her brain automatically relied on to get her through the next few minutes. "Maggie Caddel. War correspondent. *American Military News*."

Name. Rank. Serial number. It'd become a mantra of sorts. Something to help her disconnect from her body when she needed it the most. But she hadn't needed it since... Since Jones pulled her out of *Sangre por Sangre*'s headquarters. Maggie forced her eyes—too heavy—to split. And was immediately assaulted by a circle of electric lanterns and flashlights.

"I know who you are, Ms. Caddel." A calloused hand framed her chin, directing her gaze to a face on the brink of sliding right off. It felt too low, as though gravity was winning. Age defined small eyes and creased lines horizontally across the man's chin. Some sections were deeper than others. She'd never seen that before. A tall forehead tried holding onto a receding gray hairline. Though the man keeping her head upright hadn't lost much elsewhere. An open collar hinted at a spread of chest hair. Perfectly manicured. It went with his expensive-looking suit. This was someone who saw himself as important. "Damn it, lieutenant. You hit her too hard. She can barely get herself going. How is she supposed to tell me what I want to know like this?"

"Sorry, sir. We had to move fast. One of Socorro's operatives—Beam—caught us off guard. She wasn't as easy to take down as we estimated." Movement registered off to the left, and a second outline came into view.

That voice. She recognized it between bouts of dread and panic. The bonfire. He'd been there. He'd burned her SD card in front of her along with the bodies of his military brothers and sisters. Maggie tried to take in the gunmen poised with weapons clutched close to their vests. Six of them. All at the ready for their next order. "Scarlett."

"Ah, there we go. She's coming around." Sir… Whatever-His-Name dropped his hold on her face, and her neck dipped forward. He was getting his suit dirty crouched in front of her like this. Probably have to throw it away, but something told her keeping himself clean had been the plan from the beginning. Dirty work wasn't his forte. "I asked you a question a minute ago. Do you recognize me?"

How could she not? It was her job to recognize him.

His face had been smeared across news cycles for weeks leading up to the Pentagon's annual contractor review. Senator Collin Hawkes had branded himself New Mexico's savior against the drug cartels. Zero tolerance. Bigger sentences. More aggressive policies. He was a husband, a father, a grandfather even. Not only campaigning for companies like Socorro Security to operate under stricter guidelines and laws—under his control, funny enough—but proposing the military step in against the cartels slowly strangling this state one town at a time.

And he was a liar.

Because now she knew the truth. Everything that'd happened in the past week—the murder of those soldiers, her abduction and torture by Sosimo Toledano, the cover-up—it'd all come from him. He didn't give a damn about the people affected by the drug cartels. He just wanted the glory of taking them down. And she wasn't going to give him anything. "Maggie Caddel. War correspondent. *American Military News.*"

A burst of laughter popped from the senator's mouth as he struggled to turn and face the men and women at his back. "Somebody get this woman to answer me."

The soldier—the one on her left—stepped forward. Pain ripped across her scalp as he jerked her head back by a fistful of hair, but it was nothing compared to the blade pressing against her throat. "You're going to want to lose the attitude, Maggie. This isn't the kind of guy you want to mess with right now."

"You think killing me will do any good?" She couldn't stop her own laugh from rocking through her chest. More features clarified and bled into her awareness as her vision adjusted to the brightness of the lights. No masks this time. Seemed the soldiers who'd destroyed the evidence of the ambush weren't too worried about her identifying them now. Most likely because they were going to kill her. No one was coming. Scarlett might've had the chance to call in the cavalry after they were attacked at Maggie's apartment, but Socorro and Jones had made their position clear. They weren't in this fight. This was something she had to do herself.

It was then she realized where she was, and her confidence shook loose. She was in that same room. Zip-tied, at the control of others. Only this time she understood why she was here. And that her captors were afraid of her. Maggie forced a deep breath to counter the alarm signaling through her defenses. "You might've gotten rid of the photos and the bodies, but you couldn't get to me in time. I wrote the story."

She directed that to the senator. "How you sent ten American soldiers to their deaths during an operation they thought would hurt *Sangre por Sangre*. How you ordered a highly trained military unit to get rid of the bodies and kill the journalist who could expose you, then slaughtered cartel members to cover it all up. It doesn't matter that I don't have proof or that you'll probably get rid of my body the same way you got rid of those soldiers. All it takes is a nudge."

A slight shift in his jowl told her how uncomfortable this conversation was getting. That he'd underestimated how much she knew of what he'd done, and a small victory charged through her at the idea of destabilizing the man responsible for so much pain and suffering.

"You partnered with a known fugitive. I don't know the details of your deal with Sosimo Toledano, but he must've outlived his usefulness after you got your henchmen to get rid of all that evidence. So you had him killed, too. What do you think will happen once that story breaks, and his daddy learns the truth, Senator Hawkes?" Maggie gave into the needles of pain stinging at her neck from the blade. Because it was something to focus on. Something she could feel when her heart wanted nothing more than to numb itself as her left leg had done.

Heartbreak did that.

Whitewashed the mind, body and spirit of color. She'd wanted Jones to be the one to pull her back from the brink. To make her believe her past didn't have a hold on her future. And they'd gotten so close. She'd fallen in love with him. Only to once again find herself at the mercy of a man she thought she could trust. The hurt inside overwhelmed anything Senator Hawkes and his gunmen could possibly do to her physically. She'd already survived one torturer. That was the easy part. Believing in love again? That was another beast altogether.

She slipped her fingers along the structural crease at her lower back where leaking water had eroded a section of the cement floor. "How long do you think you'll last before the cartel comes for you?"

"You want to know what I think will happen, Ms. Caddel?" Senator Hawkes got to his feet, revealing an overweight frame brought on by years of serving behind a desk. Pulling a white handkerchief from his suit pocket, he wiped his hands. "I think my constituents will see I get things done. I think they'll see that I'm willing to put my own career—even my life—on the line to ensure organizations like *Sangre por Sangre* stop getting away with murder, stop pumping drugs into our schools and stop abducting our women and young girls for trade. I think they'll want action. Action that only I can give them. Because once the people of this state see how Socorro and Ivy Bardot have let the cartel grow like a cancer to bolster their bottom line, there will only be one solution—me and my willingness to do whatever it takes to win."

"It won't work." Her argument was nothing. Pathetic and weak.

"Why? Because you've written some piece that points the finger at me in the end? You're nothing but a blogger whose reputation as a bipolar schizophrenic is archived in your divorce proceedings, Ms. Caddel." The senator handed off his handkerchief to one of the gunmen as though he owned every person in the room. Maybe he did. He reached back for something from another soldier and brought it forward. Her camera. He turned it over in his hand. The lanterns glinted off what was left of the shattered lens. He thumbed the power button and a miniscule amount of light cast back onto his suit jacket. It worked. "You're right in that Toledano and I had a deal. I guess there's no point in keeping it a secret, seeing as how you're not leaving this room alive. I got word through the grapevine there was a civil war simmering inside *Sangre por Sangre*. You see, the guy at the top has let too many of Socorro's interferences slide without repercussions. Toledano kept pushing his daddy to make things right, but it turns out, the old man is more interested in profits than in remembering how he got them in the first place. So I approached Toledano with a deal that could benefit us both. All he had to do was be at the time and place I gave him and make sure nobody left alive."

"It was a setup," she said. "You got the approval for the operation by showing the military you knew exactly where Sosimo Toledano would be and at what time."

"Yeah. Well, Toledano didn't know the entire mission was proposed as an effort to guarantee his capture. He learned about that later. The second he slaughtered those soldiers, he'd signed his death warrant. There was nothing he could do or say to get out of us coming for him. And it worked out, too. Two birds with one stone. Toledano and his men were brought to justice, and now I've proven Socorro doesn't have the resources or the motive to get the job they were hired to do done. I win on both sides. Took some doing to make sure that nobody figured out what I was up to. Altering satellite footage is harder than it looks. Not to mention making sure no one got wind of the fact that Toledano left you alive, but it all worked out in the end." The senator fanned his hands out as though he'd just golfed a perfect round without having to cheat. "I was hoping you were smart enough to back off once I asked your editor to cut you loose, but I see I'm going to have to get nasty. You thought three days with Sosimo Toledano were rough? It's nothing compared to what these guys will do to you once I give the order."

"All this for me? I'm flattered." Maggie dug one finger into the hole in the floor growing bigger at her insistence. A shard broke away, and she gripped on to it with everything she had. He was right about one thing. There was no way she was getting out of this room alive, but she sure as hell was going to fight until her last breath. She'd make it hurt, too. Make sure her remains held on to a bit of their DNA.

"I think we're done here." Senator Hawkes handed off the camera and nodded to the man with the knife at her throat. He backed off, sheathing it before he stepped back. "The photos you took are gone, Ms. Caddel. The bodies of those soldiers will never be identified, let alone recovered. It'll be hard for the families, sure, but I'll be there for them. Make sure they're taken care of. After all, it's the least I can do for their sacrifice in this war."

"You're a monster. You're provoking the cartel, and they'll retaliate. Only the next set of American lives taken might not be under your control." He had to be stopped. Before this went any further. She pressed the shard through the zip ties. The plastic broke free. Maggie launched herself off the floor with the cement blade in hand and arced it directly toward the senator's neck.

Only the makeshift weapon didn't make it that far.

The soldier to the left caught her wrist.

"Heroes are overrated, Ms. Caddel." The senator stared at her from behind the tip of the shard. "They don't have the guts to do what needs to be done."

THE SUV'S TIRES skidded across graveled asphalt with a scream.

Jones threw the transmission into Park and shoved himself free of the vehicle with Gotham launching from the cabin behind him. Two Albuquerque PD patrol cars angled inward on either side of the front door. Two hours. Every second she was out there was another second she might not make it home. And he couldn't live with that.

He rounded the hood of the SUV, taking in the four-story apartment building planted just west of Albuquerque's Old Town. Gray stucco and clean lines nodded to the state's heritage, while electric neon paint brought the structure into the modern century and attracted millennials who preferred to work from home. Over-size windows stared out over the park across the street and the botanical gardens on the other side. The place came with a hell of a view, and, for a split second, Jones couldn't do anything but imagine Maggie building her new life here. Searching each balcony, he tried identifying Maggie's apartment, but they all looked the same. Her commitment and desperation to make journalism her life wouldn't have left time or energy for her to decorate, yet he couldn't help but want to believe her place was the one with the planter holding on to the remains of an underwatered houseplant.

Something new to signify the life she wanted to build.

Scarlett rushed through the glass front door leading into what Jones assumed was the building's lobby, and the rest of the world caught up in a rush. Blood dried in a crusted line down her face at the left side. But it was her freshly busted knuckles that told Jones his teammate had fought like hell to protect Maggie. "Any word?"

"No. You?" He anticipated the security consultant's answer before she shook her head. Scanning the property, he mapped out where he would've set up shop and waited for a target to walk into the cross hairs. The building itself wasn't large. At least not compared to a few others going up in the area. The park didn't provide any cover. The sons of bitches would've had to have seen Maggie and Scarlett coming to get the jump on them so quickly. He headed for the lobby. "Tell me what happened."

Scarlett brought both hands to her hips as though she was trying to catch her breath after sprinting long distance. "I did everything I was supposed to, Jones. I swear to you. I walked her upstairs and cleared the entire apartment. I checked all the windows and the back door and clocked any surveillance cameras. There weren't signs the place had been broken into. But I figured this wasn't over, that even though we were ordered to stand down, she was still in danger. So I followed protocol. Only it wasn't enough. Once I cleared the apartment, I left her there. Alone. I got back to the car, and I noticed the parking garage arm stuck open."

They pushed into the stairwell and climbed the three floors before entering Maggie's apartment. A small round dining table greeted them just inside the entryway with a terrace straight out the back door. With a single hanging planter holding onto a dying fern. The rest of the place was neat, bright and bare. They turned into the main living space, bypassing a massive kitchen island. Square cubby bookshelves lined the wall floor-to-ceiling and held stacks of books, magazines and notebooks. A desk—too large for the room—held as many, if not more, articles and notebooks. And photos.

"They stayed out of sight until they got eyes on her. Most likely through the building's camera network. Once they saw you leave, they came from the garage." Pressure accumulated in Jones's gut as he shuffled through surveillance photos. Shots of men on corners, each dated over the past year with bright sticky notes. Not professional in the least. Scribbled handwriting crossed out and rewrote theories as to the identities and movements of one subject in particular. *Sangre por Sangre* soldiers. Maggie had spent months following and identifying low-level members of the cartel before winding up in their hands. This was where her obsession had started.

"I got off a couple rounds before they put her in one of their vehicles." Scarlett's voice shook, spiking his blood pressure higher. There wasn't much that could rattle one of the best security consultants in the country. But losing a client didn't sit well with any of them. This wasn't about cushioning their bottom lines, Pentagon contracts or employment security as Senator Hawkes was determined to gut them for. This was about protecting those who couldn't protect themselves. Of penance for the sins of their pasts. "I was so focused on getting to her, I didn't see they'd left a man behind. He clocked me when I came around the corner. I held my own for a few minutes. I imagine that's what they wanted so they could get away."

"It wasn't your fault, Scarlett. These guys knew exactly what they were doing and when to strike." He forced himself to focus on the rest of the apartment and not how being in this personal space unsettled him in ways he didn't want to think about. This place was a step into Maggie's world, where he didn't have control of any of the variables. Her abduction happened because of him. Because he'd crumbled at the idea she could be taken from him as Kincaide had, that he wouldn't be enough to protect her. And he'd proven himself right by not choosing her over Socorro's and Ivy Bardot's agendas sooner. He'd let her slip from his fingers, and now she was going to pay the price.

He'd been so careful not to get close to anyone over the years that he'd honestly never saw Maggie coming. Her competitiveness to prove herself, her warmth despite having a cartel try to break her in every way. She was easily distracted by new leads, overthought everything and put all of her self-worth into goals she had no control over, but those were the things that made her unique. That set her apart from the other women in his life. She wasn't perfect, but Jones didn't want perfect. He wanted Maggie. He wanted her stressed-out workaholic approach, her inability to stick to a routine and her need for approval from others. He wanted everything she disliked about herself and more. Because he loved her.

"Security footage is no good. I already tried. Bastards destroyed the system on their way out," Scarlett said. "I found the guard unconscious in a maintenance closet. Cops are getting his statement now, but so far, he hasn't been able to identify a single member of the team that took her."

And they wouldn't. Scarlett had already proven that any nosing into military business would put them in a set of cuffs with a court date set in the far distant future. They didn't have that kind of time. They had to come at this from another angle.

"We don't need to identify them." Jones tapped the edge of Maggie's desk. He had experience with deconstructing operations, reworking them and putting the pieces back together. Iteration was key across enemy lines, improving one thing at a time over the course of a mission until you got the result you wanted. A journalist with no prior professional experience had managed to start at the bottom and work her way up. "We just need to locate them. Put in a call to Senator Hawkes's office. I want to know where he is today."

"The guy trying to get our Pentagon contract terminated? You think he's involved?" Scarlett pulled her phone from her pants pockets. The shiner in her left eye was swelling by the minute, but Jones knew her well enough, she wouldn't let something as minimal as a scalp laceration and a black eye slow her down. Putting the phone to her ear, she cut her attention to him and flashed a wide smile. "Yes, Senator Hawkes's office, please. My name? Uh… Ivy Bardot. He's been expecting my call."

One second. Two.

"Oh, he's not in the office today. Out on personal

business. Oh, that would be great. Thank you." Scarlett shook her head, dragging the phone from her ear. She punched in a series of commands on the screen. A loud ringing filled the apartment as she set the call to speaker. "She's forwarding me to his personal cell. I can run a trace on his GPS from here."

"Don't you need a court order for that?" Jones asked.

The ringing cut short, sending the call straight to voice mail.

"Haven't you heard? Socorro doesn't live up to the same standards as the rest of the country. We can do whatever we want. It's in our contract." Scarlett tried to keep her smile to herself. The line clicked. "Bingo. Voice mail."

You've reached—

The security consultant thumbed a few more taps against the screen, drawing Jones in. She worked fast, then turned the phone toward him. "And, I'm into his phone. Easy peasy. I can do anything from in here. Want to send a bunch of dirty messages to his contacts list and see how they respond?"

"I want his location, Scarlett. Now." Nervous energy tightened the muscles down the backs of his legs. Maggie was in the hands of a man desperate to destroy every shred of evidence of how he'd overstepped his authority. How long would he leave her alive? "We can send the messages after Maggie's back in our protection."

"Got it. I guess he's not smart enough to put his phone in airplane mode when he's in the middle of an abduction." Scarlett's smile fell as she handed off the phone. The blue dot signaling the current location of the senator's phone swelled and relaxed. Right in the middle of the one place Jones never wanted to step foot in again. "You think she's there?"

"There's only one way to find out. Get your gear and call in the rest of the team." Jones took one last look at the apartment, envisioning Maggie back at her desk, working on her next story when all of this was over. They were about to officially declare war on the US military. But the realization didn't come with the sense of dread he expected. He was going after Maggie. He was going to bring her home. And he'd take down anyone who got in his way. "We're going to need them."

Chapter Fourteen

"The only reason you're still alive is because I need to make sure you didn't share your little theory with anyone else." Senator Hawkes added some distance between them as his military henchman twisted Maggie's arm behind her back. Wouldn't want to get any blood on that suit, after all. "As much as I believe what I've done here is perfectly within justification for the greater good, I can't have anyone else coming out of the woodwork, you see."

A groan escaped up her throat, but she kept it from leaving past her lips. She wasn't going to give them the satisfaction. Any of them. She tried to wrench her arm out of his hold, but bone-deep pain warned of dislocating her own arm. "Well, let's see. There's my editor, who you bullied into firing me. There's the founder and operatives of Socorro Security. You know, the people who have been making sure I stay alive the past few days. Alpine Valley police, who've offered to clean up the mess you left behind on the other side of this complex. Oh, and that little circle of friends I curated at every news outlet in the country."

The senator lost a bit of that smugness etched into

the corners of his eyes. He turned to face her fully, waiting for the punch line to drop. Only she didn't have one. "You're bluffing."

"I'm not." Maggie savored the victory despite the oncoming suffering. Every cell in her body wanted relief. To be out of this room, to go home, to see Jones walk through that door as he had that first time and take her away from all of this. She tried to breathe through the pain igniting in her shoulder socket. "I'm sure you've been monitoring my email accounts. Check my outgoing folder. You'll see I'm telling the truth."

"Give me my phone." Senator Hawkes reached back without taking his eyes off her, and one of the soldiers behind him produced the device. Thumbs touched with a bit of swelling at the knuckles thumped too hard against the delicate screen. Shock swept the arrogance from the senator's expression. If he hadn't already been washed in light from the surrounding lanterns, she would've sworn he'd lost all the blood in his face. "You bitch."

"After you had my editor fire me, I started collecting a long list of news outlets I want to pitch stories to in the coming months. Bodhi was scared. I could hear it in his voice, and I didn't think that was ever possible." Her chest ached at the intersection of her pinned arm and torso. So much so, her nerve endings started tingling. Just as they had in her leg. Maggie tried to force as much oxygen into the strangled limb as she could, but it was no use. "I figured someone with a lot of authority had threatened him to drop me as one of the magazine's writers, but the evidence I'd gathered didn't pose any threat. All I had were pieces of a bigger puzzle that didn't make sense. No big picture. But whoever was behind this wanted me taken out of that picture so much they sent a highly trained military unit who doesn't question orders. Just follows them. Turns out, I was onto something. So you can tell me that your constituents and the Pentagon will support you after this all gets out, Senator. But I know the truth. You're scared of losing everything you've worked for. And now you know how it feels."

The strike came so fast, she didn't have time to brace herself.

Pain ricocheted through her face and twisted her head to one side. Her vision battled to catch up as lightning struck behind her eyes. Maggie recovered quickly with the telltale salty taste of blood. A small cut stung as she probed her tongue through her mouth, and she spat a mouthful at the senator's shoes. He wasn't just going to have to get rid of that suit. "And you hit like a five-year-old."

Senator Hawkes closed the distance between them. "You think you have any leverage here? I've been telling the media what it can and can't do since I took office. None of this is going to make a difference, Ms. Caddel. People might be upset over the next few days, but they'll change their minds once they see my results. They'll beg for me to oversee further action against the cartels. I'm going to be their poster boy. And you… You'll be nothing but a has-been who never really was. A one-hit wonder. Everyone you love, everyone you care about is going to forget you even existed by the time I'm finished."

A twinge of fear cut through her as the past week with Jones infiltrated the moment. Was that true? Would he forget her? Would she be the assignment that went wrong but had little effect on Socorro's overall mission? All she'd ever wanted was to be important to someone. To matter. She hadn't always gotten the attention she'd wanted from her parents or siblings growing up, but that'd been life. Three kids split by four years each demanded different levels of interest from two working parents trying to cover the monthly bills. She'd had friends, sure, but nothing concrete that lasted past high school. Marrying her high school sweetheart after she graduated college started to fill that hole constantly begging for her attention, but within a year, she'd noticed the signs of isolation. Of snide comments on her appearance or how she talked to his friends. Of his expectations of her growing more disciplined and intense. Of never being good enough for the man she'd married. Even during her tenure for *American Military News*, she'd been shoved to the back of the queue compared to the more veteran reporters.

But with Jones… Everything had been about her. Which sounded so selfish, even in her own mind, that it physically made her cringe. For once, she hadn't been the one trying to hold everything together. She'd been allowed to eat what, when and however often she pleased without waiting for a nasty comment about her figure. She'd rested without feeling lazy or guilty and put herself and her recovery first for the first time… ever. And he'd let her. Encouraged her. Showed her what real kindness looked like, and that asking for what she needed was the bravest and best thing she'd ever done for herself.

No. He couldn't forget all that. She wouldn't let him. Because she was getting out of here. She was going back to Socorro to show Jones how he'd changed her from the inside out. He was going to know how she felt.

A steady pulse pounded through the right side of her face, but Maggie could still make out a bead of sweat at the senator's temple. Along with the slight deepening of his voice. He was trying to stay in control. And losing the fight. "If you're so sure my article isn't going to ruin you, then why are you sweating?"

Senator Hawkes pulled at the lapels of his suit jacket to straighten some invisible wrinkle. "Get her out of my sight. I don't want to know the details but make it quick. I've got a review committee meeting to prepare for and a press release to write."

"Yes, sir." The soldier at her back hauled her against his chest.

A rumble rolled through the room and dislodged dust from the crevices along the ceiling.

She felt the vibration from the front of her foot to the back charge up both legs. Silence pressed in through the room as the dust settled against the broken-up floor.

The senator raised both hands out in front of him as though he'd found himself on some kind of balance beam. Or the ground under his feet was about to swallow him whole. "What the hell was that?"

An uneasy feeling swept from one soldier to the next. They widened their stances in preparation, but nobody knew what was coming.

She did. Socorro was coming. Jones was coming. For her. "You're going to want to start running now, Senator. I'd hate for you to meet my partner face-to-face when he's in a bad mood."

The senator didn't waste a single second. He motioned to the soldiers in his immediate vicinity. "You five, get me the hell out of here. And you—" He nodded to the gunman holding Maggie captive as Hawkes dashed for the door. "Finish this. That's an order."

"Yes, sir." The soldier's grip tightened on her arm, cutting off blood flow. "Move."

Her left toes caught on a raised section of floor, and she stumbled forward. Shards of damaged cement and gravel bit into her palms. Maggie took a moment to catch her breath.

"Get up." The soldier kicked at her heels. "Or I'll make you get up."

Pressure at finding herself once again at someone else's mercy built until it cut off her air supply. Jones and his team were still working their way through the building. It'd take them minutes, maybe an hour before they found her, especially if they were forced to stand off with Hawkes's men. By then, it'd be too late. She had to do this herself. Because no amount of self-worth could really come from the people around her. She had to have it for herself first.

Maggie fisted a handful of the debris detaching from the structure every second. It wasn't much, but it could make all the difference. She arced her arm over her shoulder and twisted her upper body with everything she had. The debris shot straight into the soldier's face.

His growl echoed through the room a split second before a burst of gunfire exploded from his rifle.

She ducked and covered as she shoved herself to her feet.

Then ran like hell.

She'd never had the chance to map out this section of the compound when under Toledano's watch. Low punctures of gunshots registered as she turned right. Heading toward the action would give the senator the chance to finish what he'd started.

Staying alive until Socorro found her. That was all that mattered. Maggie headed in the opposite direction, away from the promise of safety, away from Jones. She skimmed her hand along one wall and bolted down the corridor.

Her left leg worked overtime as the steady thump of boots grew louder. She couldn't outrun the shooter. She couldn't fight him, but she sure as hell wouldn't give him the satisfaction of finishing his mission. Maggie ducked into the nearest room as another vibration rolled through the building. Seconds ticked off as she pressed her back to the wall, out of sight of the door into total darkness.

"It's nothing personal, Maggie," the soldier said. "We're all just following orders here."

Her breathing sounded overly loud. She tried to swallow the too-hard thud of her heartbeat in her throat. In vain. He was going to find her, and she'd have to fight back.

"I know you're in here." His voice sounded much closer now. Too close. "You're all alone. That team you think is going to save you? They ain't coming in time. I told you. Nothing stops me from following orders."

Maggie searched for something—anything—to use as a weapon without giving away her position. But this room seemed just as bare as the one she'd been held in.

"She's not alone." That familiar voice cut through the corridor and through the fear squeezing around her heart. Jones. Gotham's growl followed. "And neither am I."

THE MASKS HAD come off.

But that went both ways, didn't it?

The soldier responsible for making sure Maggie disappeared turned that rifle onto Jones. Lieutenant Jason Snow, six tours in Iraq and Afghanistan, two medals of valor, on the hook with the senator who'd sent him to take the fall.

Jones could practically feel the laser sight moving from his belly to his chest. It was okay. He had one on him, too. Gotham shook waiting for permission to lunge, despite not training for combat purposes. Turned out, the dog had gotten fond of having Maggie around this past week. They were in this together. Determined to get her out alive. And they weren't leaving without her. "My team already has Senator Hawkes in custody, lieutenant. The only way you get out of this unscathed is if you let her go."

"And break orders?" The voice wasn't as high and tight as it had been at the bonfire. More strangled and smoky. As though the son of a bitch had swallowed a lungful of mold and was choking on it granule by granule. Good. He deserved to suffer for what he'd put Maggie through. "Must come so easy for you at this point, Driscoll. What is this, the second—or third—time? Any good soldier knows his own hubris can get the people he cares about killed."

"The army only minded the one time. Lucky for me, I have a new unit now. One that would do the same thing for me. So I'll do what I have to today to ensure every single one of us makes it out of here alive." And he should've done it sooner. Maybe if he'd taken a stand with Ivy before Maggie had left headquarters, they wouldn't be here. Then again, it was because of her they now knew who'd signed Maggie's death warrant in the first place.

"No. You won't." The statement was punctuated by a pull of the trigger.

"No!" Maggie shot from the darkness, hiking the barrel of the soldier's rifle upward. Strobes of light lit up the corridor in millisecond increments and revealed her fight to get control of the weapon.

He couldn't take a shot. Not without putting her in his own cross hairs. "Stay," he commanded Gotham.

The gun ripped free of her hand. "You know. I said this wasn't personal, but now it is." Snow rocketed a fist into Maggie's face. She twisted and slammed into the wall behind her before slumping to the ground. Unconscious.

Jones launched forward, weapon up. One squeeze of the trigger bolted Snow's shoulder back. The groan of pain lasted a split second as Jones descended to get control of the rifle. A spray of gunfire exploded in a long line, missing Maggie by mere inches. "You're going to pay for that."

Jones slammed the end of the rifle into the wall where Maggie had made contact. An arm navigated around his neck and shoved him sideways. They struggled—bare strength versus strength. Jones ducked to relieve the pressure on his neck and maneuvered out of the hold. Only to put his back to his opponent. Rookie mistake.

Strong arms secured around his neck and squeezed.

Latching onto Snow's wrist, he tried wriggling free. To no avail.

Snow growled in his ear, out of breath and wheezing. "Accept it, Driscoll. You've gone soft since your discharge. All this—everyone you love, everything you care about, that team of yours—soldiers like me are the ones who made it possible. You never deserved any of it in the first place."

Leveraging his foot against the opposite wall, Jones launched them backward. He slammed Snow into the cinder block behind him, but it didn't have any effect on the bastard's hold. He fell to one side in an attempt to dislodge the stranglehold around his neck as pinpricks of white moved into his vision.

Only, a section of the floor fell away.

Gravity knotted in his gut a split second before pain exploded. They hit the level beneath as one. His entire body felt as though it was about to snap in half but somehow held together. Gotham's bark echoed down through the opening they'd created overhead. Jones could just make out the husky's outline through the floating debris.

Snow took the brunt of the impact but didn't seem to miss a beat as he locked his ankles around Jones's front and squeezed to push the air from Jones's chest. "Maggie's taken one too many hits to the head, Driscoll. What do you think the chances of her waking up after what I just did to her are?" The son of a bitch pressed his mouth to Jones's ear. "Mission complete, traitor."

No. She was alive. She had to be. Because if she wasn't… He'd never forgive himself. He'd have to live with another life ruined because of his unwillingness to move when certain situations asked him to bend, and he couldn't take that weight anymore. In the end, Kincaide had been a ghost of the brother who'd stood up for him that day after school. Maggie deserved better than that. She deserved everything he had to give and more. To be happy. He could make her happy. Dust created a veil of thickness around them, almost sparkling in the beam of their dueling flashlights. She was right there. Within reach. He just had to get to her.

He tried for his sidearm. Only he couldn't pull it free with Snow's leg pinning the weapon to his thigh. Jones locked his hand around his attacker's wrist and put everything he had into getting free. The soldier's arm broke its deadly grip. He rolled out of Snow's reach then launched himself onto the son of a bitch's back. Both arms cut off Snow's oxygen. Just as the lieutenant had done to him. He struggled to stay in place as Snow bucked underneath him, wild as a bull pissed as all hell about the cowboy trying to get him under control. Strangling sounds bounced off the walls around them, but Jones wouldn't let up. Not yet.

Snow kicked at the floor and managed to bring his upper body high enough to twist Jones back against the wall. The lieutenant clawed at his hands. His groans were getting weaker as oxygen burned in his lungs.

A few more seconds. That was all Jones needed.

The soldier's boots scuffed against the floor, carving out valleys in the piled layers of dust created over the past few minutes. It wouldn't do any good. It was Jones's turn to put his mouth to Snow's ear. "Some things in this world are more important than orders, Snow. One day you're going to figure that out. But if you come after us again, I'll kill you. I give you my word."

Snow didn't get a chance to answer as he went limp.

Shoving the soldier's body off of him, he checked the lieutenant's pulse. Weakened, but steady. The bastard would live. Though what kind of life waited for him up top, Jones couldn't say. He had a feeling Senator Hawkes wasn't going to go down alone. He'd drag everyone with him to take some of the heat off, including the very men and women he'd used to start a war.

Gotham's bark intensified as the husky pawed at the edges of the hole raining down dust on Jones. Agitated at being separated from his handler. Hell. The fight was over, but time was still running out. Jones jumped as high as his body weight would allow, but his fingers only brushed the edge of the cavity. He wasn't going to make it on his own. He swiped at the dust accumulating in the air. This room seemed to be separated from the entire compound. No way in or out. And Maggie needed him out. "Get Scarlett, Gotham. Go get Scarlett. Bring her here."

The dog disappeared from the opening, his collar echoing down the hall.

"Maggie!" There wasn't any answer, and Jones's entire body was all too aware of the fact Snow might be right. That she'd taken one too many hits and wouldn't have the capability of getting back up this time. And it'd be his fault. Jones dropped his chin to his chest as the heaviness of that possibility stabbed through him. "Maggie, if you can hear me. I'm sorry. I gave you my word that I would protect you until the end of this, and I failed. I backed out on you when you needed me the most. But the truth is, I was scared. Breaking orders is what got my brother captured in the first place, and I didn't want you to end up like him. Because I love you, Mags. I've been in love with you since the moment I pulled you out of this hellhole that first time, and I saw what you'd survived. You're strong. A hell of a lot stronger than me. I don't know how you do it, to be honest, but I want to be strong for you. Just give me another chance."

"Oh, that's sweet, Driscoll." Snow struggled to get one knee under him as he grappled with the rifle strapped around his chest. "Please, don't let the fact I'm about to kill you get in the way of telling her how you really feel."

Jones unholstered his Taser, took aim and fired it into Snow's inner thigh. The lieutenant fell back harder than expected, his entire body at the mercy of forty-thousand volts. "I wasn't talking to you."

A whimper escaped up Snow's throat, and Jones took pressure off the Taser's trigger.

"Please, Mags. Say something. Tell me you're okay.

That after everything we've been through, I'm not the one who got you killed." He studied the opening in the ceiling. Only silence answered back. Then scraping. Something hesitant and steady. A hand clutched onto the crumbling shards of cement and rebar and pulled Maggie into sight.

Blood matted her blond hair and spread down one side of her face. But, hell, she was the most beautiful thing he'd ever seen. She dropped her hand, reaching for him. She wasn't strong enough to lift him out on her own, but that didn't stop him from locking his hand in hers. Her smile made him believe everything would be okay. That they could move past this, and he hadn't screwed everything up. That they could build a life—

"I love you, too, Jones. And thank you. For everything. For saving me in more ways than I can count. I owe you my life. But you did break your word, so I'll see you back at Socorro headquarters."

She slipped free of his hold and got to her feet, still unstable. He was prepared to catch her if she fell through, if needed. But Maggie simply backed away on her own strength.

"Wait. Are you joking?" He waited for an answer. However distant. For something to tell him she wasn't going to leave him down here as some kind of punishment until the team could get him and Snow out of this hole. "Maggie?"

"She ain't joking, man." Snow shook his head.

Jones pulled the Taser's trigger a second time and let the electric nodes do their job. "Still wasn't talking to you."

Chapter Fifteen

"Great. I'll look over the contract and get back to you tomorrow." Maggie disconnected the call, a smile tugging at one corner of her mouth as she reviewed her full email inbox. The offers hadn't stopped. There were contracts waiting for her review, pitches for articles to write. Voice mails from Bodhi begging her to call him back. The excitement hadn't let up since the moment she'd walked out of the *Sangre por Sangre* headquarters on her own two feet. Once the major news outlets had gotten hold of the piece she'd emailed, it seemed the entire world had opened up for her. She had her pick of assignments for a multitude of outlets if she wanted.

She was someone important now. A commodity everyone wanted.

The story hadn't stopped spreading. Senator Hawkes did exactly as she'd expected: run with his tail between his legs. The state police had picked him up just before he'd crossed into Mexico. The last she'd heard, his lawyer was going to earn every single penny of his retainer. Corruption charges waited on the horizon, along with a bunch of little ones the attorney general thought up along the way. Turned out the senator's constituents and fellow officials didn't so much agree with his attempt to undermine the Pentagon's choice in private military contractors or antagonize the cartel's kingpin by having the man's son murdered as much as he thought they would.

Maggie cut her attention to the news cycle across the room. And there he was. Being led by police out of a dark SUV and marched, in all his glory, in front of every camera in the state in cuffs. She rubbed at the cuts still stinging around her wrists. The wrinkles around those small pea-like eyes seemed deeper than the last time she'd seen him. Good. This was just a taste of the sleep he was going to lose over the next few months.

She hit the power button on the remote and turned off the TV.

As for the military unit at Hawkes's command, she hadn't been able to get much information. From what she understood, charges against Scarlett Beam had been dropped, but anything more than that had been deemed classified. It didn't really matter. This was one story she was happy to move on from. But the soldiers who'd sacrificed their lives on the senator's lie were still waiting for identification. Still had families in the dark. It would be a few more weeks before the crime lab in Albuquerque would have DNA results—if any had survived—but now that the truth was out there, she couldn't help but think this case had slipped to the top of the queue.

The dying plant on the back terrace swung with a gust of wind. Damn. She'd hoped to keep that one alive. Though having been abducted, then navigating the investigation was a good reason to forget to water. Shoving away from her desk, Maggie cut to the kitchen and pulled a small plastic cup from the cupboard. Her leg tingled as feeling returned in small increments every day. Most likely a benefit of slowing down and letting the inflammation in her back calm down instead of running from one threat to the next. She filled the cup with water from the filter in the refrigerator and wrenched the sliding glass door back on its track. Dry heat seared across her skin, and she was grateful for the sensation. Grateful to be feeling anything at all. "You're looking a little rough, my friend."

This plant was supposed to be a visual reminder to take care of herself. To not let her obsession to move forward and climb that worldly ladder get the best of her. A symbol of the new life she wanted for herself after the divorce. She pried dead leaves from the base of the plant and replaced them with a healthy serving of water. When she thought about it, humans were basically houseplants. They needed sunlight, water, love. Her heart constricted for a fraction of a second at the thought of leaving Jones down in that hole for his team to recover. She wouldn't have been able to pull him out herself. Not in her condition. But his plea— his attempt to fix things between them—followed her into her dreams every night since the final showdown. "Sunlight and water we're good on. But we're really sucking it up on the love part, aren't we?"

Because there hadn't been any contact between her and Socorro since Dr. Piel checked her over after the fight with Senator Hawkes and his gunmen. The laceration cutting across her temple was shallow enough to not need stitches. Just a whole lot of rest, considering how much she'd been knocked around. First by Toledano, the accident, then trying to escape the senator and his men. Seemed becoming Socorro's primary war correspondent had been taken off the table. She didn't blame Jones. She didn't blame any of them, really. But she couldn't ignore the void in her chest either. The one that hadn't hurt so much over the past couple weeks. While she'd been with Jones. Gotham, too. There was something about that oversize fuzz ball that'd settled her relentless drive for more.

A knock echoed from the front door.

Hope lodged in her throat as she turned back inside. Maybe she'd spoken too soon. Maggie crossed to the front door, ready for whatever waited on the other side.

Except for the man standing at her doorstep.

"What… What are you doing here?" The words lost their power at the mere sight of her ex, and Maggie couldn't help but hate the part of herself that feared him.

"Holy hell. It's true, isn't it? Everything they're saying on the news. That you were abducted and tortured by the cartel, that you uncovered that senator's plan to kill those soldiers. I can't believe it." Her ex-husband reached for the bandage at her temple, and she backed away. His hand froze, midair, as though reminded that he had no right to touch her. He retracted his closeness. Like a turtle ducking back into its shell. "Damn, Maggie. When I heard…"

She shook her head. She didn't need his pity. She didn't need him at all despite that little knot in her stomach telling her this was a familiar connection, that anything was better than nothing. Fortunately for her, Maggie recognized that healing wasn't a one-and-done kind of decision. It would take months, if not years, to unlearn those self-sabotaging behaviors. She just had to hold strong. "How did you find me?"

"My brother still works for the power company," he said.

"You had him look into me." Right. Not stalkerish at all. "What do you want?"

"I came here… You know what? I don't really know why I came here." Her ex shoved both hands into his slacks. The polo shirt straining around his upper body said he still spent way too much time working out rather than on things that actually mattered. "I tried reaching out, but you didn't return any of my calls. Guess I deserved that."

And a whole lot more. Maggie crossed her arms over her midsection, barring him from any idea he was invited inside. She could do this. Hell, she'd stood up to Toledano. She'd faced off with a US senator threatening her life. She'd even fought a soldier bent on burying her somewhere she'd never be found. "Well, I'm still recovering from what happened, and I have a lot of work to sort through over the next few days. If you don't mind, I need to get back to it."

She moved to close the door.

"Maggie, wait." His hand snapped against the wood. Too loud in the quiet hallway. The sound jarred her into fight-or-flight mode, and she instantly diverted her attention to the can of Mace attached to her keys on the entryway table. "I just wanted to explain why I said all those terrible things about you to your family. For the arrest. Looking back, I can see where it all went wrong. I got some bad advice from my business partner, to the point all I could see were dollar signs. Everything became about money, and because of that, I treated you like a threat. It won't happen again. I give you my word. Please, Mags. I want you to come home."

He was kidding. This had to be a joke.

"Your word. Somehow I don't believe you, seeing as how you couldn't even manage to squeeze an actual apology in there. You didn't come here to apologize. You came to justify what you did, and I deserve better than that. Unfortunately, I didn't realize that sooner in our marriage, but there's no way I'm coming back to you. Now get your hand off my door." Her fingers bit into the thin wood, ready to slam it into his nose if needed.

Apologetic husband disappeared from the surface of his expression. Replaced by that oh-so-familiar disappointment she was used to having directed at her. Her ex wedged his foot against the door to keep her from shutting it in his face, and she slowly reached for the Mace a few feet away without tipping him off. "Maggie, I'm trying—"

"I believe the lady told you to get your hand off the door." That voice. It filtered through the overwhelming chaos of the past few days and buried itself in the bruised parts of her body until she felt as though she could lift a truck with her own two hands.

"Who the hell are you?" Her ex physically took a

step back as all six-foot-something of Jones Driscoll stepped into her vision. No Kevlar, no sidearm, but just as prepared to take on another fight of hers if she let him.

"I'm the man who's going to watch her rip that arm from your body and shove it down your throat if you don't do what she says." Piercing gray eyes found her, and the world burst into a variety of color. "You good, Mags?"

"I'm good." Maggie fisted Jones's T-shirt and dragged him over the threshold, and he came all too willingly. His body heat swept through her at that mere contact between them. Not missing a beat since they'd last seen each other. She liked that. The little threads of electricity he seemed to charge inside of her. She turned her attention back to her ex. "Thanks for stopping by."

Then shut the door in his slack-jawed face.

"I'm never going to forget this moment or how good it feels." Maggie pressed her back against the door, trying to catch her breath. "That man has made me feel like less than the dirt under his feet so many times. It felt good to show him he doesn't affect me anymore."

"Glad I could be of assistance." Jones's half smile smoothed from his mouth as he closed the distance between them. "Now let's talk about how you left me to rot in that hole."

HER BREATH SHUDDERED through her. Unbalanced but confrontational. Not in the least threatened or intimidated by him. And, damn, it was good to get this close to her again, to see her on her feet and fighting for herself. "To be fair, I thought your team would know they needed to pull you out. It wasn't until I got to headquarters that I realized they'd taken their time."

"Six hours, to be precise." The feigned frustration was starting to slip. Though he'd lost count of how many times he'd had to tase Lieutenant Snow while they'd been stuck in that hole, he hadn't once let himself put the blame on her. He'd deserved to rot in that compound for backing out of his promise. "Seems Gotham isn't too good at following orders, either. Instead of bringing Scarlett back, he started wrestling with Hans and Gruber once the action had died down. Forgot all about me."

She tried to contain her laugh, shooting one hand to her mouth, but failed. "I'm sorry. I know it's not funny, but at the time, I was still dazed by what'd happened and you'd said all those things about being in love with me. I couldn't think straight. I just needed to step back, take a few days to get my head on straight. But look, you made it out. Call it even?"

The break in her composure loosened that tightness in his chest that'd formed while not hearing from her over the past few days. Maggie Caddel had finally put herself and her well-being first, and he couldn't fault her for that. "All right. I guess I can give you that, considering you're the reason I didn't get sprayed with a bunch of bullets."

"See? Compromise. That's how relationships are supposed to work," she said.

"Relationships?" The word pricked at the back of his neck. "Is that what this is? A relationship?"

Maggie set her palm against his chest, and an instant shot of ease tendrilled into his hands and under his rib cage. Stepping into him, she added to the hint of warmth churning from merely getting this close. "Did you forget about the part where you said you loved me, and I said I loved you, too?"

"I was in a hole for six hours. I had nothing else to think about. Well, other than arguing with Snow every time he wanted to kill me down there, but that's beside the point." His hands found her hips, holding her steady. "Maggie, I failed you. I did the one thing I swore to you I wouldn't do. I let you take on this battle with Hawkes alone, and I'm going to spend the rest of my life regretting not standing up for you sooner."

A heaviness pulled at his stomach. "I almost lost you down there. When you didn't answer me, I thought I had, and the feeling gutted me. I don't know how else to explain it, except that the thought of not having you in my life hurt more than losing my brother ever did. That's not to say I didn't love him or that I don't miss him. I do. I just love you more, and, after everything you've been through, I hated myself for being the one to hurt you. I'm sorry. I'm sorry that you had to be the brave one and save my ass in the end, and I will do whatever it takes to prove to you that you can rely on me from here on out. Anything you want. I'm here. As long as you'll have me."

"You didn't fail me, Jones." Maggie pressed her front to his, and something clicked. Like a piece of himself that'd been missing for a damn long time had finally been put back in its place. "And, you're right. For once

I had to be brave, and the weird thing is, even though I could've died, I'm grateful. Because I had to realize I've let the past control me all this time. I thought I'd left it behind once the divorce papers were signed and I started this new career, but I see now all the hurt, all the pain and the lies still had a grip. They were what drove me to obsess about being better and proving I didn't need anyone, and I don't want to live in spite, Jones. It's exhausting, and it's giving power to the wrong people. People I don't even like. And after I saw that soldier take aim at you—ready to kill you—in that corridor, I knew what I had to do. I couldn't let those things have a space inside me anymore. There just isn't room now that you're a part of my life, and I like the change. It makes everything I've been through worth it."

Hell, he loved her so damn much. They might've only kissed for the first time a week ago, but he'd fallen in love for what felt like a lot longer than that. "So where does that leave us?"

"I'm not sure." She shifted her weight between both legs, and the left seemed to support her a lot better than it had a few days ago. She was on the way to healing. In more ways than one, and he couldn't help but feed into that nodule of pride of her standing up to her ex as she'd done. "I have offers coming in every hour. Some from across the country. They all want to hire me, even the big guys. CNN, FOX, *The New York Times*. It's a lot to consider, but I didn't want to make a decision about any of them until I had a chance to talk to you."

"Maggie, you don't need my permission to take a

job, even if it is across the country," he said. "Whatever you choose, I'll support you."

"I know, and believe me, for the first time, I wasn't looking for anyone's permission but my own. But the past couple of weeks, even though they contain some of the most terrifying moments of my life, were a lot more manageable when you were around." She fisted her hand into his T-shirt. "I think that's something worth exploring. I meant what I said in that compound. I love you. I know it doesn't make a whole lot of sense considering what we survived together—or maybe it's because of what we survived together—but it's true. I'm not the same person you rescued that night. I'm stronger, I'm braver, I'm more willing to stand up for myself. Because of you. I wouldn't even be considering taking one of these jobs if you hadn't shown me who I really am and what I deserve for myself. And I think I want to keep you around."

She smiled then. Really smiled. That smile that only ever seemed to come out with him around. There was a spark she liked to keep buried and refused to show the world, but with him, Maggie lit up his whole damn insides with a mere glimpse of it.

"That is the most romantic thing anyone has ever said to me." He notched her chin higher and set his mouth against hers. He kissed her all the way through the kitchen and the living room, nearly ripping her clothes off her body on the way. Jones didn't get to take much of her bedroom in before he found himself flat on his back against the mattress and Maggie falling into bed with him. Her hair skimmed across his chest once she finished tossing his shirt somewhere out of sight. "I want to keep you around, too."

Maggie was someone he hadn't let himself want. Not just because she'd been a client he'd sworn to protect, but because he couldn't put himself through another loss. But stripped down like this—physically, emotionally—with her, Jones couldn't see any other way of going on living. As though she should've been at his side his entire life. One break in the seam of his lips, and he was utterly devastated. By her. And damn, he'd give anything to keep this feeling.

"I want to stay." Her words brushed against the underside of his jaw. "Here in New Mexico. Bodhi has offered me my job back. Well, begged really, and I'm going to take it as long as our deal still stands. You being my source and me having exclusive access to Socorro."

"Ivy's having the paperwork drawn up as we speak," he said.

She couldn't contain her smile. "Then I'm going to stay, but I want to leave the city. I want to live slow and enjoy this new chance I've been given instead of trying to survive one incident to the next. With you, Jones. I know you have to stay on-site with Socorro as long as you're contracted to work for them. So what would you think of me moving to Alpine Valley to be closer to you?"

A buzz of desire thudded hard under his skin as she peeled away to look down at him. He understood what she was asking, what she was willing to give up, but Jones couldn't make the dots connect. She had everything going for her right now, and she was willing to give it all up. For him. "Are you sure?"

"Yeah. I'm sure. I can submit pieces I'm working on to the other outlets on the side or take on freelance jobs as long as I have the room in my schedule. The cost of living is lower in Alpine Valley in case I decide to take a few vacation months here and there. That's the beauty of working from home. And you won't have to change anything. You can still go out there and protect the people who still need Socorro. *Sangre por Sangre* took a beating the past couple weeks, but I feel like something big is coming. And I want to be there. With you." She kissed him, deep and soft at the same time. "Besides, I'm pretty sure it's going to be hard to travel back and forth across the country with Gotham."

His growl drove him to flip her beneath him. The sad truth was the dog would leave with her in a heartbeat. That was the kind of effect she had on the people— and K9s—who cared about her. They were willing to give up their whole lives for the slightest chance she'd make them feel like this. Supported. Loved. Whole. "He's technically Socorro's property. You'd have to take up any custody disputes with Ivy."

"Does the same apply to you?" Trailing her fingers along his jaw, she seemed to memorize every inch of his face as though she'd never seen it before. "Am I going to have to fight for you again? Because I'm telling you, I'm feeling pretty good about my chances now that I've got experience."

"No, Mags. I'm yours." And he meant it in every way he hadn't thought possible before. Jones had convinced himself his heart had died in that cave with Kincaide's mind, unwilling to give up his armor. Only now it seemed the key had been surrendering to Maggie, and there was no going back. Not ever. "Forever."

"We have a new deal then." She kissed him again. "Forever."

* * * * *